*Pool of Tears*

# POOL OF TEARS

## JOHN WAINWRIGHT

ST. MARTIN'S PRESS   NEW YORK

Library of Congress Cataloging in Publication Data
Wainwright, John William, 1921-
    Pool of tears.

    I. Title.
PZ4.W1418Po3   [PR6073.A354]   823'.9'14   76-62797
ISBN 0-312-63008-5

Her first idea was that she had somehow fallen into the sea ... However, she soon made out that she was in the pool of tears which she had wept when she was nine feet high.

Lewis Carroll
*Alice's Adventures in Wonderland*

# MONDAY – OCTOBER 26th

11.15 am . . . . . .

By no moderate stretch of the imagination could the woman be called beautiful. She was not even pretty. She was ordinary, but her very 'ordinariness' was of such a degree that it set her apart; it was so complete – so absolute – that it made her almost unique. She wore chain-store clothes, and the clothes fitted her well enough, because she was 'standard size'. The colours were browns, greens and russets; autumn colours ... not because it was autumn, but because these were the colours she always wore. Her hair was short (once, it would have been described as 'bobbed') and had the sheen of good health and conscientious care, but its cut was almost simple enough to merit the term 'severe'. She wore minimal make-up; a touch of lipstick and a light patting of face-powder ... no more.

She knocked, and entered the study carrying a spiral-backed notebook and newly-sharpened pencil.

She began, 'Mr Adams, I think you should ...'

'Ah, yes, Miss Benson, I'm glad you've come.'

He was prematurely grey (almost all-over white) and, some people thought, uncommonly young for the weight of responsibility he carried. The tips of his fingers were still touching the receiver of the desk telephone. He was frowning; part-annoyance, part-worry ... one of those frowns

7

which carry a not-of-this-world vagueness, peculiar to over-worked academics.

She said, 'Mr Denning sent word you wanted to ...'

'Emmerson,' he interrupted. The frown took on more depth, and he said, 'Peter Emmerson.'

'The coloured boy?'

'He's in Mr Finchley's class, isn't he?'

'Yes.' She nodded. 'At the moment, they're on Technical Drawing.'

'I've just had a phone call.' He glanced at the instrument and, at the same time, removed his fingers from the receiver and began to massage the muscles behind, and below, his right ear. He continued, 'From the hospital. His father's had an accident.'

'Oh, dear!'

'... He apparently stepped off the kerb. Something of that nature. I understand he's severely injured.'

'He's – er – he's a widower ... isn't he?'

'Ye-es. That's the problem.' Adams lowered his hand from the side of his neck. He fiddled, old-maidishly, with folders, rulers and pencils on the surface of the desk, as he went on, 'There's no other next-of-kin ... as I understand it. Just the boy. There's also the possibility – the *bare* possibility – of it being fatal.'

Miss Benson said, 'Oh, dear!' again.

Adams suppressed a sigh, and continued, 'The hospital authorities think he should be there. They're very insistent.'

'Of course.'

He stopped fiddling, looked up at her, and said, 'I, personally, don't see the necessity, Miss Benson ...'

'Surely. His father ...'

'... He can do no good. It will merely upset the boy ... far more than he *needs* to be upset. The kindest thing would be to let him know. As quietly as possible. Even

8

underplay it, a little. Then, when school closes, we can arrange for him to visit the hospital, this evening.'

'And, if his father dies? Before this evening?' she asked.

'One must be optimistic, in these circumstances,' he said, heavily. 'He may not die. The chances are, he *won't* die ... one must not allow emotion to get the upper hand, and cloud the facts.' He moved his shoulders, resignedly, and ended, 'However ...'

'You'll want to see him, of course.' She made as if to turn, towards the door.

Adams said, 'Would you mind arranging for a taxi, first?'

'Yes. Of course.'

'The number's – er ...' He glanced at a scribbling-pad, alongside the telephone. 'Five-four-two-one-three.'

'Five-four-two-one-three,' she repeated. 'I'll phone from my office.'

'Then, ask Mr Finchley if he can spare Emmerson, for the rest of the afternoon. Ask him to send him to my study, as soon as possible.'



12.30 pm ......



Nathaniel Emmerson had a secret. It was the greatest secret in the whole, wide world; the most superb – the most impossible – the most breath-taking secret *ever*.

Jesus!

And, having thought the word, he was sorry for *having* thought the word because, taking The Lord's name in vain was a poor way of giving thanks for such a blessing. And *such* a blessing!

9

It made up for just about everything.

It made up for his skin, and the fact that a lot of whites still called him 'nigger', and a lot of coloureds still called him 'Uncle Tom'. It made up for years of bad life; for years of serving drinks, from behind the concert-room bar, at *The Blue-Tailed Fly* – of being part of a strip-cum-clip-joint – of being blessed (or, maybe, cursed) with the magical touch of drink-mixing and, because of this expertise, being forced to watch helpless, while good, decent girls (white and coloured) were fed into the vice-machine and ended up Jezebels and (more often than not) diseased Jezebels.

He'd tolerated it – he hadn't *enjoyed* it, but he'd tolerated it – for the sake of Pete ... and for the memory of his beloved Daisy.

He'd promised Daisy. He'd look after Pete – he'd make sure he grew up a good boy – no matter what it cost. And *The Blue-Tailed Fly* paid good money. It wasn't *clean* money but, in a place like that, there was a lot of it – and plenty more, where *it* came from – and, when they found a man (or a woman) who functioned well, and with real craft, they weren't mean.

But (oh, brother!) this secret. Another week – maybe two, no more than three – and *The Blue-Tailed Fly* could look around for another bar-keep. He'd be out. Him and Pete. Maybe a chicken farm, somewhere; a *real* chicken farm – not one of those battery-hen factories – where the chicks scratched around and the cockerels strutted amongst their lady-loves, and the air was clean, and Pete could grow up big, and strong, and ...

Nathaniel Emmerson dreamed dreams, and chuckled quietly to himself, as he cracked eggs into a basin, as the first step towards making himself a mid-day omelet.

He called, 'Come right in,' to the knock on the door.

The girl from the greengrocer's shop, opposite, poked her

head round the door, and said, 'You're wanted on the phone, Mr Emmerson.'

'Dammit, the number of times I've told folk ...' He stopped, grinned an apology, and said, 'Sorry, Judy. I shouldn't swear, in front of ladies.'

'That's okay, Mr Emmerson.' She returned the grin. 'I've heard worse.'

'Tell Ted I'll be right over.'

She said, 'I'll do that,' and closed the door.

He wiped his hands on a tea-cloth, before following her across the street.

In the shop, he said, 'I'm sorry about this, Ted. I keep telling folk this ain't my phone. Asking 'em not to put you to all this trouble. I keep ...'

'In the back, Nic. You know where.' The greengrocer smiled his friendship, and jerked his head towards the rear of the shop. 'It's off the hook, waiting.'

'Anyway ... thanks. I'll tell whoever it is not to do it again.'

'No bother.'

Emmerson trod his way past opened crates of cabbage and stacked sacks of potatoes, carrots and Brussels sprouts. The tiny storeroom smelled more earthy – more 'countrified' – than the countryside itself. It was a basic smell. The smell of soil, the smell of vegetation; the smell of growth and life; the smell of genuine freedom.

Emmerson sniffed, appreciatively. He loved that smell ... he just *loved* it. Every time he entered the shop – and, especially, if he had an excuse for visiting the rear storeroom – he savoured that lush scent of living earth.

There was a desk tucked away in a far corner of the storeroom; a repository for bills, invoices, V.A.T. returns and the like. It was an old desk – rough-used and dirt-marked – and it held an unfiled shuttering of paperwork which, in turn, was also rough-used and dirt-marked. It also held a telephone, and the receiver of the telephone was off its rest and atop one of the piles of forms.

Emmerson lifted the receiver to his ear and spoke into the mouthpiece.

He said, 'Nic Emmerson, here.'

The voice was muffled, as if it spoke through the folds of a handkerchief.

It was a man's voice, and it said, 'Emmerson. Listen carefully. I'll not repeat what I'm going to say. We have your son ... do you understand that?'

'P-Pete. I – I don't ...'

'We *have* him,' said the man's voice. 'Check ... but check quietly. Call the police, and we'll notify you where his grave is. We're serious, Emmerson. You'd better believe that. It'll cost you thirty-thousand to see your son alive, again. And you'd better believe *that*. We'll be in touch.'

There was a quiet click, then the soft purr told Emmerson the phone was dead.

1.50 pm ......

'Who?' Adams looked nonplussed.

'Mr Emmerson. Peter Emmerson's father.' Miss Benson looked equally perplexed.

'But – I thought ...' Adams left the sentence incomplete.

'I told him to wait in your study.'

'Did you – er – mention ...? The message we received from the hospital? What we've been led to understand?'

'No.' She shook her head.

'What – er – what does *he* say? Does he offer any sort of explanation?'

'No. Just that he'd like to see you. Urgently.'

'This is ridiculous.' Adams sounded annoyed. He began to close, and fold, his day's copy of *The Observer*. 'Does he – er – does he *look* as if he's been involved in a road accident?'

'No.' Once more, she shook her head.

Adams repeated, 'This is ridiculous,' moved a plate to make room for his folded newspaper, dabbed his lips with a napkin, muttered a quick apology to his neighbours and stood up from the refectory table.

He hurried along corridors, and mentally composed the words he would say to Emmerson. Phrases of mild outrage. Terse remarks; to the point and, while skirting actual offensiveness, leaving no doubt about the annoyance of an overworked headmaster confronted by time-wasting ...

Time-wasting *what*?

He was curious. It would be interesting to hear what empty excuses this coloured bar-keeper would come up with.

Adams entered the study, and Emmerson stood up from a chair.

As he closed the door, walked to the desk and waved Emmerson back to his chair, Adams said, 'I find this visit inconvenient, Mr Emmerson. Inconvenient, and very puzzling.'

'Yes, sir,' muttered Emmerson.

As he lowered himself into the desk-chair, Adams said, 'My information – at about eleven-fifteen, this morning – was that you'd been involved in a road accident.'

'Oh!'

'Against my better judgement, I arranged for a taxi to take your son to the hospital. To see you. They were very adamant. They assured me you were severely injured.'

'N-no, sir. I ain't ...'

'I can see you're not and, if this is some sort of jape – some sort of hoax – I find it extremely ...'

'It – it ain't a hoax, Mr Adams,' stammered Emmerson.

'Indeed?'

'No, it – it – it ...'

Emmerson's eyes carried the dead look of shock. His voice was little more than a hoarse whisper, and the words soaked into silence and disappeared, like spots of rain on parched earth.

'Well?' demanded Adams. He stretched a hand towards the telephone. 'I think a complaint to the hospital authority is called for. If they've made a mistake of identity it shows a very lax ...'

'No!' Emmerson jerked forward in his chair. The impression was that only sudden will-power prevented him from snatching the telephone from Adams's reach. 'It – it ain't a mistake, sir. It ain't the hospital's fault.'

'Really?' Adams lowered his hand onto the desk top, and waited.

Emmerson blinked his eyes, and rubbed the back of a hand across his lips, before he spoke and, when he did speak, there was near-incoherence and a pleading urgency to be believed in his voice.

He said, 'Yeah ... there was this accident, sir. Weren't much. Weren't much, at all. But – but I reckon they thought it was pretty bad. More bad than it was ... see? Just – just a bruise ... that's all. But – but I reckon they thought it was more. They – they *did*. They – they thought it was real bad. But, it weren't. That's – that's why.'

'Why they sent for your son?'

'Yeah.' Emmerson nodded, eagerly. Breathlessly. 'That's – that's why they sent for him, sir. Because they thought it

was bad. A lot more bad than it was. Not just – y'know
... a little old bruise. They – they thought it was *real*
bad.'

'A very odd mistake to make,' mused Adams. 'An unusu-
ally bad diagnosis.'

'Yeah.' Once more Emmerson's head bobbed in eager
urgency. 'Th-that's what I said, Mr Adams. That's what I
*told* 'em. Sending for Pete, like that. It – it ain't right. It –
it ...'

Emmerson dropped his head, rested his chin on his chest
and, for a moment, almost accepted defeat.

There was a few seconds of silence, before Adams asked,
'Where is he now?'

'Eh?' Emmerson looked up.

'Your son, Peter. Can we expect him back at school, this
afternoon?'

'We-ell – er – no, sir. I reckon not.' Emmerson swallowed,
then repeated, 'I – er – I reckon not, sir.'

'Why?'

'He – he took it bad, Mr Adams.' Emmerson stumbled
through the thicket of forced lies. 'Y'know ... we're pretty
close. Since his ma died, Pete and me are pretty close. So,
he took it bad. That's – that's why I reckon he – he'd best
not come back to school, today. He's – he's resting ... see.
I reckon that's best. T-to let him rest up a while.'

'Tomorrow, then?' smiled Adams.

'Yeah – well ... maybe. See what – what ...' Emmerson
fluttered his hands, helplessly.

'What a night's rest can do.' Adams ended the sentence
for Emmerson.

'Yeah. See what he's like, tomorrow.'

'Not too long, Mr Emmerson,' said Adams, sternly.
'Don't pamper the boy.'

'Oh no, sir. I ain't likely to ...'

15

'And, please remember, *any* interruption in his education can only do harm.'

'I'll – I'll remember that, Mr Adams.'

Adams stood up from the desk, and held out his hand. Emmerson, too, stood up.

They shook hands, and Adams said, 'Thank you for letting us know, Mr Emmerson.'

'That's – er – that's okay, sir. I – y'know – figured it best that you *should* know.'

As he held the door open, Adams smiled, and said, 'Good afternoon, Mr Emmerson. Tell Peter we'll be expecting him back at school, as soon as possible.'


2.10 pm . . . . . .


Bordfield Regional Metropolitan Police District Head-quarters.

Strictly speaking (and if external appearances were anything to go by) it should have had its name blazoned, in coloured neon, above its maw-like entrance, and with the words 'Bingo Hall', or 'Bowling Alley' added. It was that sort of a nick. Originally (before the amalgamation shake-up) it had been Bordfield City Police Headquarters; when Bordfield had been a county borough, with a population of around the half-million mark, with its own cops and its own police authority; before the city of Bordfield, and the slightly larger city of Lessford, plus God only knew how many square miles of the surrounding county, had been lumped together to form one bumper-family-sized, damn-near-unmanageable, monumentally barmy Metropolitan Police District; before the loons at Whitehall had seen fit to

16

doodle meaningless lines all over a map ... before *that*, it had been Bordfield City Police Headquarters.

And the city elders (of the original Bordfield County Borough) had had some rather kinky ideas.

The building was impressive – much like The London Hilton is impressive – much like the B.B.C. Television Centre is impressive ... but *not* as a police station. Not even as a police headquarters. It was about six times too big, with about twelve times too much floor-space. It needed an army of cleaners, and could well have used its own, private North Sea gas rig as a means of providing fuel for its central heating system. It had rooms – quite a few rooms – for which a use could not be found. It even had *some* rooms which, after the initial conducted safari, following the mayoral opening, had been firmly locked ... and, moreover, had remained firmly locked, ever since.

It was a white elephant – strictly speaking, an 'off-white' elephant ... a very grimy, and annually becoming *more* grimy, 'off-white' elephant.

Some architectural crackpot had dreamed up a vision of straight lines and flat surfaces, constructed in beautiful white stone; of a virgin monument to his own short-sightedness; of a structure which would dazzle the eye and blind the onlooker ... at least, until the muck got at it!

The belch from the city's factories, brickworks and chemical plants had kyboshed *that* dream, in no time at all.

It was now streaky and tatty-looking ... like a pale-faced, over-grown tart, who'd been caught in a downpour and whose mascara had run badly.

It was an eyesore.

The coppers grew to live with the eyesore. Indeed, the coppers grew to live *in* the eyesore. At first, they loathed the place – their nostalgia blinded them to the hundred-

and-one shortcomings of their old Number One Nick, where both men and paper seemed to have been spilling from every door and window and where corners of semi-privacy (much less purpose-built interview rooms) where they might hold heart-to-heart talks with miscreants were at a premium – but, gradually, they realised the truth ... that a man with ten acres of good growing-ground need not, necessarily, plant every square inch with lettuce. The trick was to use what you want, *for* what you want, and hold the rest in reserve.

The Bordfield Regional Metropolitan Police District Headquarters was, therefore – and despite its external appearance, its size and its echo-proneness – a moderately well-liked 'manor house'.

It had a Telephone Exchange Room, with a switchboard Houston Space Control Centre might have envied.

The copper working the switchboard had been on duty a mere ten minutes – he was girding his not inconsiderable loins for the prolonged bind of a two-ten shift – and, already, he was having trouble with a lunatic on the other end of a telephone wire.

'Missing?' said the constable. 'How do you mean, *missing*?'

'We don't know where it is. That's what I mean.'

'Y'mean it's been pinched. A stolen car ... is that what you're reporting?'

'We-ell – no ... I wouldn't say pinched.'

'What *would* you say?'

'Lost. Y'know ... lost.'

'A taxi?'

'We've been trying to raise it, on the air, for the last two hours. More.'

'And?'

'Nothing. Not a sausage.'

'Maybe his radio's on the blink,' suggested the constable.

'He should have been back here, more than an hour ago.'

'All right. Maybe he's broken down.'

'Look.' The voice from the taxi firm was impatient. 'I have it here, on the log. Last two calls. To pick up a fare, at seventy-five Fairfax Avenue, for the bus depot ... that was at ten-fifty hours. Then, we drummed him up on the radio, at eleven-twenty, to pick up a fare at Gladstone Comprehensive, for the City Hospital. After that, nothing.'

'Tried the hospital?' asked the constable.

'Yeah. They can't help ... taxis arrive there, all the time.'

'Who's the driver?' The constable picked up a pencil and moved a pad of message forms to within writing distance.

'Len Garfield. One of the part-time blokes.' There was a pause, then the question, 'Any accidents that you know about?'

'No. Not so far, today. Not in the Bordfield area.'

'Where the hell *is* he, then?'

The constable said, 'Let's have a few details. I'll get it circulated ... but let's know, if he turns up.'


2.20 pm ......


The flimsy from the Telephone Exchange Room reached the Radio Control Room, and read –

MESSAGE. TIME RECEIVED 14.10 HRS.
MORRIS 1100 HACKNEY CARRIAGE — BLACK — REG. NO.
UGX. 9986.T — MISSING FROM FIRM 'CITY TAXIS' —
WHEREABOUTS UNKNOWN — RADIO CONTACT LOST —
DRIVER, LEONARD GARFIELD.
REQUEST OBSERVATION FOR THIS VEHICLE BY MOBILE
UNITS, BORDFIELD AREA.
NOT — REPEAT NOT STOLEN VEHICLE.

The sergeant in charge of the Radio Control Room scanned the text of the message, sniffed mild disgust, and said, 'We've had lost dogs, lost kids and lost handbags. That I can understand. But, to lose a bloody *taxi*! ... that takes real genius.'

He handed the flimsy to a policewoman constable.

The policewoman strolled across the polished floor, made herself comfortable on a swivel chair, positioned a goose-necked microphone to within four inches of her lipstick, flicked a toggle and read the contents of the flimsy into the microphone for the edification of fifteen patrolling squad cars.

2.35 pm .......

Emmerson had seen it done, so often. On the T.V.; on the afternoon repeats of multifarious cops-and-robber sagas, put out by the television people for the benefit of evening-workers and bored housewives; in the auditoriums of darkened cinemas, where a yawning matinee performance lost money, but did a little to combat the eternal loneliness of a handful of 'senior citizens'. He'd read about it — not

20

often, he was no great reader, but the few books he *did* read invariably included this sort of situation ... and it had always seemed so off-the-cuff easy.

In fiction, it *was* easy.

In one door, and out of the other. Over a handily-placed garden wall. Along a convenient alley. Onto an expediently slow-moving bus.

It was toffee-apples ... the way *they* did it.

But *they* weren't doing it for real. And *they* knew who was after 'em. And (the clincher) *they* didn't have Pete to worry about.

Emmerson was a very simple man; very uncomplicated ... as was his faith. He believed in God. Emmerson's God, moreover, was a very matey deity; a very down-to-earth type, to whom Emmerson could chat in everyday language. Emmerson's God was not the God worshipped by bishops and archbishops. Emmerson's God was a sort of glorified Father Christmas; a benign, and smiling, Creator who cheerfully tossed the odd miracle into the scheme of things as His contribution towards making life a little less difficult; who (as long as you didn't take too much strong liquor, swear too often, or mess about with wild women – or, if you weakened and did such things, repented later) patted His followers on the head, put His arm around their shoulders and assured them that the Walking-On-Water trick was just a warm-up ... the really *fancy* stuff was theirs for the asking.

Before he left the house, Emmerson had a very serious conversation with his God.

After that, it *was* easy ... and the real thing, too!

He walked down the street, caught a bus, bought a 10p ticket then left the bus at the next stop. A hundred yards from the bus stop, he hurried into a public toilet and didn't even reach the stalls before he turned round and hurried out again. Woolworths was next; in, through the swing-

21

doors, a quick zig-zag around the counters, then an exit through the door he'd entered by, followed by an about-turn, back into the store and a slow jog-trot to the rear exit. After that came the pedestrian precinct; a warren-like mix of paved walks and shop frontages; ideal for Emmerson's present purpose and, for almost thirty minutes, he turned, twisted and doubled back in the approved James-Bond–Mike-Hammer manner.

By the time he'd left the pedestrian precinct, sprinted to the bus terminal and jumped aboard an already-moving bus to Lessford he was breathless . . . and almost dizzy.

But, he was satisfied. Nobody had followed him . . . nobody *could* have followed him.

The pity was, it had all been a wasted effort.

Nobody had *been* following him.

The bruise above the youth's left temple showed red, and swollen, where the length of lead-shot-weighted rubber hose had slammed home, across the plain-chocolate-hued skin. The swelling stretched downwards and caused a slight overhang to the left eyebrow. A broad band of surgical tape concealed his mouth, and kept his lips closed. His wrists were bound behind his back, with nylon twine.

Garfield held open the rear door of the 1100, and said, 'Out you get, Pete. This is as far as we go.'

The youth struggled, awkwardly, to leave the car.

From the rear seat, the bruiser who'd been his escort planted a foot in the small of the youth's back and pushed. The youth stumbled and Garfield caught him in his arms, before he sprawled in the inches-thick muck of the stackyard.

'Steady, boy.' Garfield's smile was friendly. He cupped the youth's elbow, and led him towards the farmhouse, as he said, 'Nothing's going to happen to you, Pete. Nothing

too bad ... you have my word. First, some grub. Then ...
ask the questions, and I'll answer 'em.'


**3 pm** ......


Emmerson didn't like Lessford too much. It wasn't like
Bordfield; it was more sprawling, slightly bigger and, therefore, slightly less 'human' ... and, of course, it wasn't
'home'. And, another thing (a very odd thing), it always felt
a few degrees colder at Lessford than it did at Bordfield; an
overcoat colder ... it didn't matter what the season (Spring,
Summer, Autumn or Winter) it was *always* an overcoat
colder at Lessford than it was at Bordfield.

Emmerson shivered as he walked from the bus station,
and sought a telephone kiosk.

Having found a kiosk, he checked his supply of 10p pieces
before looking up the S.T.D. code number. Zero-five-one-
two-three-six. The first six figures to an 'open-sesame' number which would link Emmerson to a personage whom he
trusted only slightly less than he trusted his own, individual
God.

Garfield said, 'Sorry about the leg-iron, Pete. But ... I don't
have to draw diagrams.'

'You're sure daddy's okay?' The last of the worried doubt
crinkled Peter Emmerson's forehead.

'Honest,' said Garfield. 'That was a necessary come-on.
He'll be worried – bound to be ... but there was no accident.'

'*Daddy!*' sneered the bruiser.

'What's wrong with that? He *is* my daddy.'

Garfield grinned, and said, 'Maybe he didn't have one.'

'Watch it, fink,' warned the bruiser, threateningly.

They'd eaten – the three of them – and their empty plates and used cutlery were still in position on the plain, deal-topped table. The table went with the room, and the other furniture; a flagstone-floored, farmhouse kitchen, heated by a well-stoked 'Yorkist' range; a low-ceilinged room, with age-blackened oak beams carrying the weight of the upper storey; a room whose unevenly plastered walls had once been whitened by now yellowing colour-wash. A deep, floor-to-ceiling cupboard filled one corner of the room. Shelves, of varying sizes and varying depths had been plugged into position, with no thought of an overall pattern. There was a shallow, stone sink, with hot and cold water taps, and a blue plastic bowl in which already-scummed water awaited the used crockery. The chairs were wooden – kitchen – utility ... a set of four, with the spare chair standing alongside the hearth. There was a high-backed bench – solid and uncomfortable-looking – along one of the walls; the sort of quasi-antique found in village pubs and in the vestries of village churches.

The youth's right ankle was linked to the leg of the table by an old-fashioned leg-iron. Other than that, he had complete freedom of movement and speech.

Nor did he show signs of fear, other than, perhaps, when the bruiser scowled and growled some threatening remark. His worry, concerning the condition of his father, had been assuaged by Garfield's assurances, and what remained could, at most, be described as apprehensive curiosity.

He certainly wasn't afraid of Garfield.

The bruiser pushed his chair from the table, stood up, and said, 'The car.'

'I think so,' murmured Garfield.

'Don't let the kid con you into doing anything stupid.'

'You deal with the car. I'll look after Pete.'

The bruiser grunted, and lumbered from the room.

Garfield and the youth sat in silence for a few moments. Garfield lit a cigarette, and seemed to get solace from the tobacco smoke.

In a quiet, sombre voice, the youth said, 'You won't get away with it, Mr Garfield.'

'Yes, Pete ... I think we will.'

'And, if daddy doesn't pay?'

'He will. You *know* he will.'

'Why?' asked the youth.

'Reasons.' Garfield moved his shoulders. 'A lot of reasons.'

'People like you, Mr Garfield. *I* liked you.'

'Uhuh.'

'Isn't that important?'

'Being liked – being popular ...' Garfield sighed. 'It doesn't buy the groceries, Pete.'

'All right,' conceded the youth. 'But, why me? Why not some rich kid? Why not the kid of some rich father?'

'You *are* the kid of a rich father, Pete. Remember?'

'It's a rotten trick, Mr Garfield. You should feel ashamed.'

'Yeah.' Garfield nodded, slowly.

'I'm your friend ... was. Down at the Youth Centre ...'

'Pete!' There was disillusionment and self-disgust in the gently-spoken interruption. 'You're how old? – sixteen? ...'

'Fifteen. Fifteen, and four months.'

'You're bright. You know at least *some* of the answers.'

'I don't see what that has to do with the Youth Centre. You were ...'

'I was – I *am* – in my mid-twenties, Pete. In no time at all, I'll be thirty. Then, middle-aged. No time at all! I've a university degree. I'm a qualified teacher. And, what do I do? – what's the only thing I'm *allowed* to do? ... teach kids, like you, how to play table-tennis, in a crummy Nissen Hut. What the hell, Pete. What the *hell*!'

'I'm sorry,' muttered the youth.

'It's not your fault, kid. It's the system. They don't want to know about Wordsworth any more. Shakespeare's out. Browning, Blake, Milton ... who cares? These days, it's Beckett, Proust and T. E. Lawrence. Literary jigsaw puzzles ... and half the pieces don't even fit. I can't teach it. I won't try. So-o, it's helping out at a Youth Centre and part-time taxi driving ... when I should be showing kids, of your age, the beauty of their own language.'

'And kidnapping?' said the youth, gently.

'I need cash, Pete. I need a new life.'

'I think you're being very silly.'

'Maybe.' The twisted grin was part-agreement. 'With a man like him – the big man ...'

'We needed him. We needed muscle.' He nodded at the bruise on the youth's forehead, and added, 'I'm sorry about that. His sort ... they get carried away.'

'You were in the taxi, Mr Garfield,' said the youth, quietly. 'You were driving it. Whatever happens, you're every bit as much to blame.'

'We're *all* to blame. Equally.' No attempt was made to hide the bitterness and disgust. Garfield took a deep drag on the cigarette, screwed the remainder of the cigarette into the film of gravy which covered the bottom of his plate then, in smoke-wrapped words, said, 'Don't worry, boy. Nobody's going to hurt you. *I'll* see to that. You'll be back with your father, in a few days. Meanwhile ...' He stood up. 'Let's have that leg-iron off. Let's have you upstairs ... then the lady of the house can clean up after us.'

4.15 pm ......

The officers from the old county constabulary area found the taxi ... what was left of it.

The two motor patrol constables beat the fire service to the scene, by less than five minutes, but the presence of the fire service was somewhat unnecessary icing around an already ruined cake.

The Morris 1100 (what was left of it) was way and gone to hell, on the moorland tops; on a dirt road, hidden from the world by cliff-like inclines of bracken-covered wilderness. Somebody (a formal statement was duly taken) had seen the billow of smoke, from a distance; had scrambled to a vantage point and seen the blazing car; had hared the best part of two miles, to an isolated A.A. box, and dialled nine-nine-nine.

The squad car had taken the message and, after a slightly hairy ten-mile dash, had arrived in time to watch the last of the upholstery curl itself into blackened goo.

All the fire service saw was hot and twisted metal and half-hearted spirals of smoke.

'Nice,' said the fireman, drily, as he aimed foam at a point where foam was no longer needed.

'No bodies,' said the patrol cop, without emotion.

'Good ... it makes it less messy.'

'But, cars don't fire themselves.'

'True,' agreed the fireman.

'So, who's jumped the gun on Bonfire Night?'

'That's your department, mate.' The fireman aimed the foam at the boot of the car. 'There's a number plate ... if you can make it out.'

27

'It might help.' The patrol cop moved towards the wreckage.

'Not yet,' warned the fireman. 'It's still hot.'

The bruiser figured the cops were dumb. But *dumb*! That was his considered opinion, and the fact that, on four separate occasions, he himself had (obviously) been somewhat dumber than the said cops and, as a result of this relative dumbness, had spent a total of seven nauseant years breathing the confined stench of slops, carbolic and cell atmosphere, did nothing to dissuade him from this firm conviction. Cops were dumb ... every last one of 'em.

Hadn't he been here, at the bus stop, like a spare prick at a wedding, when the fuzz-wagon had belted past? Hadn't he *still* been here, when the fire-cart had followed? And, just now, the Red Cross brigade?

All this high-speed activity – all those uniformed finks ... and nobody had even *noticed* him. How dumb was it possible to *get*, for Christ's sake?

Which was a good thing, of course.

It had saved him the trouble of having to spin the old madam; of having to convince some snotty-nosed flatfoot that he, Bert Hicks, had a deep-rooted love of open spaces; that a late-October hike across damp moorland was the nearest he could ever get to a personal Paradise in an otherwise loused-up world.

You never knew, with these things ... they might not have believed him.

But, that was okay. Fortunately, cops were dumb. They hadn't even *asked*.

In the distance, the local single-decker trundled nearer along the ribbon of road. A nice, slow-moving, stop-at-every-sheep-dip, countryside bus which would, eventually, drop him off at Thirsk. And, at Thirsk, he'd pick up his own car and drive to Bordfield.

Money for old rope ... because the cops were so damn *dumb*.

In his terrace house, which formed one tiny part of one of the less affluent districts of Bordfield, Emmerson used a nail-brush and Lux toilet soap on his hands and fingers. He scrubbed hard and long, and wrist-high, and the water was hot enough to almost scald. It was the colour, you see ... and Emmerson was very conscious of the colour. Some people (a surprising number of people, in this so-called age of reason) *still* didn't like coloured fingers touching something which was, eventually, going to touch their lips. It was crazy. It was more than crazy – indeed, a grain of dignity, deep inside Emmerson, sometimes insisted that it was downright *insulting* – but the folks who used *The Blue-Tailed Fly* were customers, and customers spent money, and money was needed for wages ... so-o, crazy or not (insulting or not) the idiosyncrasies of the customers made the difference between him being in, or out of, work.

That damn grain of dignity!

Folks with yachts – folks with big houses – folks with money – they could *afford* to be dignified. They could *afford* dignity. Garfield Sobers, Muhammad Ali – a handful of men, and some women, with the wrong shade of skin – dignity was okay for them. Their choice wasn't between dignity and starvation. And why? Because their colour wasn't brown and black ... it was brown and black, tinged with gold.

A tear spilled out of each eye and rolled, slowly, towards his chin as the day's truth drove its red-hot dagger home.

Y'know ... that he could have been one of them.

That, until that telephone call, he'd dreamed that his

29

days as a bar-jerk were numbered. A nice house, in the country. Not too big – not too fancy – just the right size for him, and Pete. And enough money. Enough money for what *they* wanted; nothing fancy, nothing extravagant, nothing to make folks raise their eyebrows and sneer ... just enough. Enough for him to sit out the rest of his life in comfort. Enough for him to feel happy that Pete might get *real* equality, in a world of con tricks and snide principles.

And now, this!

Jesus ... sorry, God, he shouldn't have said that. But, Christ (sorry, again, God!) a dream comes true, you live with it for a few days – you hold your muscles in tight, to stop your stomach from fluttering around, you clamp your teeth together, to keep your mouth shut – and then *this* happens. The choice between a future *with* Pete, and a future *without* Pete. Some choice!

Unless ...

Help him, God. Y'know ... stand alongside him. He ain't like me. He ain't *sure* ... not like I'm sure. But (y'know, God) he's a good man. I don't have to tell *you* that. I'm just reminding you – not really reminding you, God ... just telling you that *I* know. That he's a good man. If anybody can do it, he can. You, and him. He's a little bitter – okay, I guess we're all a little bitter ... with this skin we've maybe something to be a little bitter about. Yeah – it's wrong – it's a sin, and I know that ... but it's a sin lots of us can't get out of our minds. So – y'know ... don't hold that against him, God. When he needs you, *be* there.

It's not that I want the money. No – that's a lie, ain't it? ... sure I want money. But not for *myself*. For Pete. I promised Daisy ... you were there, God, when I promised Daisy. And it ain't going to be too easy, keeping that promise, without the money. With the money, I can do it, God.

I can do it good – I *will* do it good ... you know me, God. I ain't big – I ain't important – I ain't got any big ideas ... except for Pete.

So, look after Pete for me, God. Don't let him be too scared.

And, if you're needed – y'know, *if* you're needed ... be around.

Emmerson turned the tap and swilled the soap from his hands and wrists. He dried himself on a nice clean towel, then used the towel to dab the stain of tears from his face.


5 pm ......


He was one of the modern crop of detective constables; collar-length hair, mutton-chop side-whiskers and drooping moustache ... the impression was that he was peeping out from behind a thicket. He was self-educated, up to the standard of two 'A' levels, G.C.E., which meant he went in for big words; he showered syllables around with joyful, don't-give-a-damn exuberance of confetti thrown at an old-fashioned wedding. The clothes completed the image, dark blue nylon shirt, with a cravat instead of a tie; corduroy jacket, belted and with zipped pockets; checked trousers and khaki coloured footwear which couldn't quite decide whether to be boots or shoes.

He was the complete 'with it' detective constable. His name was Joyce.

He said, 'Those are the circumstances, Mr Lipton. If my information is to be relied upon, it's a complete write-off.'

Lipton breathed, 'Bloody charming!' ... Lipton's education *not* being up to the standard of two 'A' levels, G.C.E.

Joyce unzipped a pocket and produced a leather-bound notebook, complete with slim, gold-plated ballpoint.

He said, 'If it's convenient, could we have relevant details?'

'Eh?'

'The person responsible for the vehicle. As I understand, his name was Garfield ... am I correct?'

'Aye,' sighed Lipton. 'Len Garfield.'

'Leonard?'

'Aye ... Leonard.'

'And his usual address?'

'Lemme see – er ...' Lipton screwed his face into an agony of concentration. 'Billings Road – no, Billings *Lane* ... twenty-five Billings Lane.'

'You're quite certain?'

'Uhuh.'

'Perhaps you'd like to consult your employees' register.'

'Er – no-o ...' Lipton hesitated, then said, 'He was – er – y'know ... casual. We used him, when one of the regulars was off sick. On holiday. That sort of thing.'

'The past tense,' observed Joyce.

'Eh?'

'The expression "we used". The expression "was off". The presumed implication being that Garfield is no longer your employee.'

'What d'*you* think?'

'I'm in no position to answer that question.'

'A Morris 1100,' said Lipton, sadly. 'They grow on trees. The insurance people fanny around ... we'll be lucky if we get *half* its market value. No ... you can say Garfield *doesn't* work for City Taxis any more. In fact, if he shoves his bloody nose in this office, after this lot, he'll get six lace-holes up his arse.'

'That should be interesting to watch,' murmured Joyce.

32

'What?'

'Contortionally speaking.'

'Eh?'

'Can we establish a few things,' said Joyce, patiently. 'A few estimated times. The last time you saw him, for example.'

'Ten to eleven, this morning,' said Lipton, promptly. 'A phoned-in call. Garfield had just arrived. He took it. Fairfax Avenue to the bus depot.'

'Fairfax Avenue.' Joyce wrote in his posh notebook, with his posh pen.

'Fifteen,' added Lipton.

'I beg your pardon?'

'Fifteen – fifteen Fairfax Avenue ... somebody called Chambers.'

'I'm obliged.'

Beyond the tiny office – beyond the picture-window, which was set into the partition-wall, separating the office from the radio room – an elderly man with an eye-patch and a badly scarred face droned instructions and addresses into a table-microphone; he gave it the appearance of the most monotonous job on God's earth ... never looking at the microphone, but keeping his unpatched eye aimed at a clipboard, on the table, alongside the microphone, and continuously adding to, or scoring out, hieroglyphics which almost covered a ruled sheet attached to the clipboard.

Joyce looked up, and said, 'Ten-fifty hours, Garfield attended to a call from fifteen Fairfax Avenue. Name of caller, Chambers ... right?'

'Right.' Lipton nodded. 'Then, we sent out a radio call, for him to pick up a kid, at Gladstone Comprehensive, and take him to the City Hospital.'

'An injured pupil?' asked Joyce.

'No ... just a kid. Emmerson. A Miss Benson – head-

33

master's secretary – phoned in the call. We wirelessed it out to Garfield at eleven-twenty.'

'This Emmerson child? You're sure he wasn't in need of hospital treatment?'

'It wasn't mentioned.'

'But, presumably, it's a possibility?'

'Ask the Benson woman.'

'An action I've every intention of taking,' murmured Joyce.

'But, it seems to me – y'know, it seems to *me* ... they'd have buzzed an ambulance, for anything urgent.'

'Quite.' A branch of the thicket stirred as Joyce raised an eyebrow. He said, 'Now – if you don't mind ... about Garfield.'

'What about Garfield?' asked Lipton, innocently.

'You hinted at "casual employment".'

'Er – yes ... y'know.' Lipton smiled a smile which wasn't a smile.

'National Insurance stamps?' murmured Joyce.

'The price of 'em!' groaned Lipton, softly.

'Not if you choose the uncomplicated way of not buying any.'

'Ah!'

'I think,' said Joyce, 'that you can expect a visit from an official from the Department of Health and Social Security, in the very near future.'

'Is it ...' Lipton swallowed, then said, 'Is it necessary? Y'know – I'm down a bloody car ... is *that* necessary, to add to my grief?'

'Both of you, I'm afraid,' said Joyce, sorrowfully. 'You *and* Garfield. I'll inform him, when I see him. You can commiserate with each other, next time you meet. Meanwhile, I require a statement. We tape as many as we can, these days, then there's a typed copy which you read and

34

approve, before you append your signature.'

'Is that a fact?'

'Shall we say ten o'clock? Tomorrow morning. I'll be available, at Police Headquarters. Just enquire at the public counter. My name's Joyce.'

'Joyce *who*?' asked Lipton, nastily.

In all sincerity, it must be emphasised that Detective Constable Joyce – despite his hirsute eccentricities and oddball dress-sense – was a fair-to-moderate police officer. He wasn't psychic. He was no crystal-gazer. He preferred coffee-grounds to tea-leaves.

This being the case, he had a series of unanswered questions ... all of which (as far as Joyce was concerned) were *going* to be answered, and none of which were in the Gordian Knot league.

A Morris 1100 (one of the fleet owned by City Taxis) had failed to answer a radio call. Later, it had been found, burned to a frazzle, miles from where it should have been.

The man who should have been behind the wheel – the man who, presumably, had driven it to the back of beyond – had *not* been behind the wheel ... nor had his grilled corpse been behind the wheel.

The two-times-two table of basic bobbying, therefore, came into play.

Find Garfield. Ask Garfield a few pointed questions. Note the answers, check the answers, verify their truth ... then hang a few charges round his neck.

It didn't even need footwork ... Joyce (being the type he was) performing most of his to-ing and fro-ing in the zippy comfort of a souped-up Mini-Cooper.

A run-of-the-mill enquiry. A nothing. A breeze. As easy as pulling birds.

\*     \*     \*

Garfield smiled at the youth. It was a very empty smile; it carried no conviction, and a good measure of worry. The youth was sprawled on an old-fashioned, Victorian iron bed; on a patchwork-squared quilt, beneath which was red blankets, flannelette sheets and a flock mattress. The youth's ankle was linked to the ironwork, at the foot of the bed, by the leg-iron.

'Chess?' suggested Garfield.

'No, Mr Garfield, I don't feel like chess.'

Of the two, the youth seemed more composed; more adult; more aware of the seriousness of the situation.

In a quiet, sombre voice, he said, 'I shall tell them who you are, Mr Garfield. When they ask me who did it, I'll tell them.'

The smile altered, and became a little embittered.

'You, and the other man,' added the youth. 'The man who hit me across the head.'

'Hicks?'

'Is that his name?'

'Bert Hicks,' said Garfield.

'So, you can't possibly get away with it, can you? If daddy *gives* you the money ...'

'He will, Pete.'

'It'll only be a loan. You'll have to give it back, when they catch you.'

'They won't catch us, Pete. It's all worked out.'

'Unless you kill me,' said the youth, thoughtfully. He looked at Garfield's face, and added, '*Are* you going to kill me, Mr Garfield?'

'Good God, no!'

'They do ... more often than not.'

Garfield walked to the window. He stared out, into the deep gloom of the October evening, and the glass of the window formed a black mirror which reflected an expression which was both tortured and determined. The bulb, with its cheap shade, sent an orange glow across the back of his neck and shoulders; like gimcrack stage lighting, emphasising the ham of a shoe-string amateur production. The dialogue, too, was ham; no self-respecting playwright would have dared to put such words into the mouth of one of his characters. Ham ... but, like a good percentage of normal, emotional language, ham for real.

He said, 'Nobody's going to hurt you, Pete. I keep telling you ... *nobody's going to hurt you*. Not while I'm around. A lot of things ... I'm a lot of things. Not very nice things. A failure. A square peg, weak, an all-round lousy individual. A kidnapper ... okay. But that's the limit. I don't hurt people ... I try not to *hurt* people. I won't stand for *that*.'

'Daddy?' said the youth, softly.

'He knows you're all right. He knows you're safe. He'll be worried ... of course he will. But, that's all. He'll soon have nothing to worry about. He'll have you back. He'll be short a little money ... that's all.'

'A *little*?'

'Dammit – yes ... *a little*!' It was a soft, self-delusory snarl. 'He's never had it. He won't miss it. He'll have more than he *had*, anyway. We're not taking it all.'

'Most of it.'

'We need it. *I* need it. This mile-high rut I'm in. It isn't even a *comfortable* rut. The only people I know are the wrong people. People I detest. Louts ... like Hicks. His sort. Drunkards. Pot-smokers. The dregs ... *they're* the kind who live in this damn rut with me. I'm souring, Pete. Inside, I'm souring. Words – poetry – they haven't the magic they once had. I'm becoming coarse. Music – even music ... it's still nice, but it isn't *necessary* any more.' He turned to face the youth and, in a voice strangled with

37

self-pity, ended, 'I need that money, Pete. I *need* it ... for the sake of my soul.'

5.35 pm ......

'Fifteen,' said Joyce.

'There isn't one,' said the man who'd answered the door. 'Thirteen – this house ... it's the last house in Fairfax Avenue.'

'Rather peculiar,' murmured Joyce.

'Not unless they're going to build a house in there, old son.' The man jerked his head in the direction of the nearby wall. Beyond the wall was the gravestone jungle of an over-filled cemetery.

'Chambers,' said Joyce. 'They gave the name as Chambers – the address as fifteen Fairfax Avenue. They telephoned for a taxi at ten minutes to eleven, this morning.'

'Nobody called Chambers lives round here.' The man frowned, and said, 'We're called Potts ... if you're trying to be funny.'

'Coincidental, I assure you.'

'It had *better* be.'

'Or,' mused Joyce, 'deliberate ... on the part of some hoaxer.'

'Not funny.'

'In bad taste.'

'Not *funny*,' repeated the man, coldly.

'Hoaxers sometimes have a devious sense of humour.'

'Oh, aye? Well, I'll bloody soon wipe the grin off his face ... whoever he is.'

'Quite.' Joyce closed his posh notebook, and said, 'I'm

38

obliged, Mr Potts. My apologies, if I've inconvenienced you.'

He turned and walked back towards his parked Mini-Cooper.

Emmerson changed into his white uniform; a newly-laundered jacket, trousers and shirt, for each evening; a black cummerbund and black bow; a fresh scarlet carnation in the button-hole of the jacket; a matching scarlet handkerchief in the breast pocket.

'Smart as paint, Nic ... as always.'

Quincey closed the door of the tiny dressing-room, as he spoke.

'Evening, Mr Quincey,' said Emmerson.

Quincey leaned with his shoulder blades resting on the panels of the closed door. As always he looked self-assured – and why not? ... he was the owner-manager of *The Blue-Tailed Fly*, and *The Blue-Tailed Fly* was one of the most popular night-spots north of King's Cross. It was popular because it *deserved* to be popular. It fed good food and good booze, at high prices, and the high prices kept the bums at bay. It put on a classy floor-show; strip, with that little extra something the also-rans lacked; never drag ... because any guy who went for a drag act *had* to be a kook, and Quincey didn't go for kooks, of whatever creed or colour. Quincey believed in good, clean filth, with plenty of sparkle and lots of limes; as long as a man's taste was straight and natural – be he a tit-man, or an arse-man – Quincey obliged.

The goods ... served in spotless surroundings and by a highly-trained staff.

That was why *The Blue-Tailed Fly* had a clientele prepared to drive anything up to fifty miles and more for a night out at Quincey's place.

'I been hearing things,' said Quincey with a knowing, not-quite-pleasant smile.

'Sir?' Emmerson straightened the cummerbund and tried to show interest; tried to hide the worry which gnawed away at his guts.

'Things,' drawled Quincey. 'That coloured hat-check bint, Dinah.'

'Miss Lemmings.'

'She's been dropping hints, Nic.'

'I wouldn't know what you mean, Mr Quincey,' muttered Emmerson.

'Ain't you happy here, Nic?'

'Sure. I'm happy here, Mr Quincey.'

'I mean really happy. Y'know ... *happy?*'

'Sure. I'm very happy, Mr Quincey.'

'No ideas about leaving?' taunted Quincey, gently.

'I'd – er – I'd let you know, Mr Quincey. You'd be the first one I'd tell.'

'Is that a fact, Nic?'

'Yes, sir.'

'Before the Dinah dame?'

Emmerson ran the palms of his hands along the wings of his greying, tight-curled hair, and said, 'I'm not – er – I'm sorry, Mr Quincey. I'm not with you.'

'About leaving *The Blue-Tailed Fly*, Nic.'

'Me?' Emmerson pretended surprise ... but it was a poor attempt.

Quincey was wearing immaculate evening dress. *His* carnation was white. He looked down at the carnation, touched its petals, gently, with manicured fingers and moved his voice down the decibel-scale until it was little more than a drawled whisper; a whisper, heavy with innuendo and encrusted with unspoken threat.

He said, 'I pay good wages, Nic. For a nigger, like you, I pay very good wages.'

'I – I don't like that word, Mr Quincey.'

'I pay to use that word, Nic.'

'I – I ...'

'I pay for a little thing called loyalty.'

'I'm loyal, Mr Quincey. Anybody tell you I ain't loyal is ...'

'Nobody auctions you away from *my* pay-roll, Nic.'

'Look – it ain't ...'

'I know some very mean men.'

'Sure. I – I know that, Mr Quincey.'

Quincey looked up from the flower, and asked, 'You got your hands insured, Nic?'

'Eh?'

'They're good hands. They can mix, and shake, good.'

'Th-thanks, Mr Quincey. I – I ...'

'Unless something hurt 'em.'

Emmerson moistened his lips.

Quincey purred, 'Hurt 'em, real bad, Nic. Y'know ... *real* bad.'

'I – I ain't got 'em insured, Mr Quincey,' muttered Emmerson.

'So-o, if they *was* hurt. Like, with a hammer. Like, with an axe.'

Emmerson gulped a shuddering breath, then stammered, 'I was – y'know ... figuring it was time I maybe retired, Mr Quincey. That's all. Just retired. I'm – I'm an old man, Mr Quincey. Since my Daisy went, I've been a lonely old man. I figured, maybe ...'

'You got a kid.'

'Pete?'

'What's he do, evenings? While you're here ... what's this kid of yours do?'

41

'He – he – he . . .' Emmerson almost broke. He swallowed, then muttered, 'Home work. He – he does his home work. W-watches the television. Sometimes, he goes to the youth club.'

'Retiring, did you say?' said Quincey.

'I was – y'know . . . thinking along those lines, Mr Quincey. Just thinking.'

'Don't set your brain alight, Nic.'

'I – er – maybe just mentioned it. To Dinah. Y'know . . . just mentioned it.'

'Think of your kid,' advised Quincey, softly.

'I – I *always* think of Pete, Mr Quincey.'

'That's nice to know.'

'Yes, sir.'

'No retiring . . . eh?'

'No, sir,' sighed Emmerson.

'Not till *I* decide.'

'No, sir, Mr Quincey.'

'And no moving to behind some other bar . . . eh?'

'I – I wasn't . . .'

'You're mine, Nic.' Quincey switched on his not-quite-pleasant smile, again. 'That black hide of yours . . . I *own* it. Right?'

'If you say so, Mr Quincey.'

'And nobody has an option. Right?'

'Right, Mr Quincey,' said Emmerson, heavily.

The smile broadened into a grin. A pseudo-friendly grin.

Quincey said, 'We're friends, Nic. That's why I pay you good. That's why we get along. Don't forget that, Nic. We're friends . . . let's *stay* friends.'

'Yes, Mr Quincey.'

'Okay.' Quincey moved away from the door. 'Go to it, Sambo. Don't keep the customers waiting.'

42

'No, sir, Mr Quincey,' breathed Emmerson.

Quincey watched him leave the tiny dressing-room and, mentally, spat his disgust.

Niggers! All that crap about 'equality' ... equality up a duck's arse. They were still plantation-fodder; thick-skulled coons who rolled their eyes and showed their teeth ... or else. Dress 'em up in a monkey suit, and they could serve drinks. Gear 'em out in something less than a bikini, and they showed shiny brown legs all the way up to their plump little rumps. They fetched and they carried – they made the guys randy and kept the dames wondering whether what was said about the black boys was true – and that's what they were worth ... and *all* they were worth.

They were a novelty ... see?

And that's why they were used at *The Blue-Tailed Fly* – and why some of the well-heeled of them were even allowed to be customers ... but that was the *only* reason.

Like the monkey, alongside the organ-grinder.

Yeah – like monkeys ... and, periodically, they had to be reminded about who provided the nuts!

6 pm ......

Miss Benson – Miss Agatha Benson – favoured Detective Constable Joyce with her undivided attention. He was, you see, such a change; such a pleasant change from a stone-deaf, half-blind mother – a sulky, demanding, overbearing mother to whom, when she wasn't at work, Miss Agatha Benson was forced to play perpetual nursemaid; such an exciting change from a never-ending diet of Trollope, or Thackeray, Galsworthy or Dickens, Coleridge or the Brontë

43

Sisters whose excellent prose Miss Benson was forced to read to her stern-faced parent for at least an hour, each evening.

Joyce was a policeman ... a *detective*.

And policemen (and especially *detectives*) were awe-inspiring creatures who inhabited a strange and breathless world; a world of criminals and even murderers; a world saturated in blood and reeking of horror; a world, the like of which Miss Benson dared hardly contemplate.

And such a handsome young man. So well-spoken. So immaculately dressed, complete with neckerchief and the modern equivalent of a hacking-jacket.

'Please sit down, sir,' she murmured.

'Thank you very much, ma'am.'

'Er – miss.'

'I beg your pardon ... miss.'

Joyce settled himself into the deep, ancient, but surprisingly comfortable armchair. It was a hell of a long time since anybody had called him 'sir' ... in fact, he couldn't remember *when*. It was a nice feeling; it warmed his ego, no end, and more than compensated for all this fannying around checking times and movements of a cheapjack, part-time taxi driver.

'Tea?' suggested Miss Benson.

'I'm sorry, I ...'

'It won't take a minute, sir. I was about to make some. I'd be delighted if you'd join me.'

'Er – well – thanks ... I'm obliged, miss. That would be very refreshing.'

'Sugar?'

'One spoonful, please.'

'Milk, or lemon?'

'Er – lemon, if it's not too much trouble.'

'No trouble at all, sir.'

44

'It's weeks – months – since I had good tea, spiced with lemon.'

Miss Benson bobbed her head – it was almost a token curtsy – before fluttering from the parlour and towards the kitchen.

It took Joyce more than two hours to get what small information Miss Benson could provide. Two very pleasant hours; two leisurely hours coaxed into the present, from an age which was long-dead.

Yes ... Miss Benson could remember the taxi calling at the school, for the boy, Peter Emmerson ... indeed, she herself had telephoned the City Taxi firm. She'd been with Mr Denning (one of the Maths masters) when Mr Adams (the headmaster) had sent for her. The headmaster had been very upset ... not to be wondered at, of course, when faced with the task of breaking such news to a pupil. What sort of news? ... oh, didn't Detective Constable Joyce know? That the father of the boy – a coloured gentleman called Mr Emmerson – had been involved in a road accident. That was what the taxi was for. To take the son – Peter Emmerson – to the City Hospital. The hospital had telephoned Mr Adams, and insisted ... although, actually, they *hadn't*.

'Hadn't?' Joyce sipped the last of his tea, and looked puzzled.

'It was a hoax,' explained Miss Benson.

'On the part of the hospital?'

'No.' She shook her head. 'We don't know who sent the original message ... only that Mr Emmerson visited the school, later in the day.'

'Today?'

'Yes. At about one o'clock. Mr Adams was at lunch. He saw Mr Emmerson, in his study.'

'But – to go back a little, if you don't mind, Miss Benson

– the taxi did call at the school? It did collect the youth Emmerson?'

'Oh, yes. I telephoned for it. Then I took Emmerson out to it.'

Joyce smiled, and said, 'I realise it's asking a great deal, Miss Benson, but can you remember the driver? A general description would be invaluable, if you could only ...'

'They called him Garfield.'

'Did they, indeed?' Joyce raised pleasantly surprised eyebrows.

'Emmerson knew him. He said something like "Hello, Mr Garfield. Are you taking me?" ... something like that.'

'But *you* didn't know him?'

'No, sir. I'm sorry.'

'Please, don't be sorry.'

'I'm afraid ...' Miss Benson simpered, slightly. 'I'm afraid taxi drivers aren't included in my circle of friends.'

'No. Of course not.'

'But young Emmerson knew him. Quite well ... or so it seemed.'

'You've been a great help, Miss Benson.' Joyce made as if to push himself from the armchair.

'More tea?' said Miss Benson, hurriedly. 'You seemed to enjoy that cup very much.'

'I did. Indeed, I did. There's an art in tea-making ... and you seem to have mastered that art, Miss Benson.'

'Another cup, then?' She glowed at the compliment.

Joyce relaxed back into the armchair, and thought what the hell. An old biddy here, asking for it – *begging* for it ... probably can't even remember the last time she dropped 'em. So-o, why disappoint her? What was it they said about old fiddles? We-ell ... why not see how much truth there was in it?

46

Screw Garfield. Garfield could wait – so could the City Taxis ... at a guess, it was some crackbrained practical joke that came adrift, somewhere.

He smiled up at her, and said, 'Why not? Why not, indeed? I've had a hard, and rather disappointing day. This is my last enquiry, before I go off duty. So, why don't I relax and enjoy your excellent hospitality?'

She almost ran from the room, and never once remembered her crotchety old mother, waiting for her daily dose of classics.

Joyce grinned to himself, in anticipation.

Those two G.C.E. 'A' levels ... at times, they tended to bring home some very unexpected bacon.

6.30 pm until 10.30 pm ......

Four hours – a mere sixth of a day ... a nothing. Two-hundred-and-forty tiny shavings from eternity, each a mere minute thick ... an eyeblink.

But, for a city like Bordfield ...

Multiply it by half a million, and you get *real* time. Year upon year of human existence. Epochs and ages – umpteen lifetimes ... and all in the space of four hours.

An army of office workers put down their pens, closed their desks and made for whichever tiny space of the city they called 'home'. The so-called 'manual workers' washed the grime of their trade from their skins and prepared themselves for an evening's relaxation.

The night people – the showbiz crowd, the projectionists, the club entertainers, the restaurateurs, the waiters, the barmen, the cinema and theatre usherettes – hurried through the October gloom, to their gaudy places of employment. The other 'night people' – the fly-boys, the prozzies, the pimps, the bouncers and all the other weirdos who figured it was easier working hard on the twist than it was working – began to watch faces for potential suckers.

The more staid of the city turned switches, and a galaxy of television screens showed coloured shadows.

The youth of the city used tubs of cosmetic – drums of hair-dressing – barrels of face-powder and talc – gallons of after-shave lotion – as they made ready to inhabit the dance halls, the disco joints, the pubs and the clubs.

It was 'transformation time'; the duckling-to-swan-and-pumpkin-to-stage-coach o'clock in this city, as in every other city and, if the 'riches' were only a little less tatty than the previously-worn 'rags', what of it? What the darkness hid from view, the coloured lights didn't reveal.

It was the four hours of the evening ... the time for all good, red-blooded men to go to the aid of some party!

And, specifically?

Garfield spent most of the evening playing Scrabble with the youth, Emmerson ... but without his mind being on the game.

It wasn't (he argued) kidnapping. Not actually *kidnapping*!

Okay, if the cops caught on, that's what *they'd* call it. But the cops weren't very imaginative. It was well beyond police comprehension to understand that this was just a way out. The *only* way out. That, in a world whose values were as cockeyed as a monkey-puzzle, there wasn't much room for a genuine aesthetic. Not for the *real* lover of beauty; the lonely, perceptive individual who could see perfection – be it in verse, or cloudscape, or prose, or the petals of a

48

flower – and, by its mere sight, become fulfilled. Become complete and know that, for one priceless moment, life held some sort of meaning.

But, where was the place for such a man? Where, in this rag-bag of economic, political, financial and industrial mishmash? *Where?* Where was the corner of privacy that didn't stink of corruption? Where was the sanctity that didn't have a plastic fence?

Not here, in this country ... that, for sure!

But, for God's sake, somewhere. *Somewhere!*

It had to be somewhere. An island, perhaps. An island, with a silver-sanded beach. An island, with a silver-sanded beach, and a palm-tree-lined shore, where the muck of the world hadn't yet reached and where packaged-tourism hadn't yet sullied with its commercialised trash.

Ten thousand could get him there. Ten thousand – his share – could melt the walls of this invisible prison in which he was captive. Melt the bloody walls, and give him freedom. Freedom to search, freedom to find and, eventually, freedom to live.

So – what the hell the cops called it – it wasn't kidnapping.

It was *escape.*

Garfield ... he spent most of that evening playing Scrabble with the victim of a kidnapping which, by means of twisted self-indulgent logic, he almost convinced himself *wasn't* kidnapping.

He lost at Scrabble.

And (if the truth be known) he didn't do much better in the game of self-kidology.

The man paced the hearthrug of his heavily mortgaged, detached bungalow and, in a voice as cold and as smooth as any icicle, spat controlled fury at the oaf who had the impudence to speak to him in such a manner, and in his own home.

He said, 'Mr Black, you will kindly moderate your language.'

'The hell I will!'

'You're angry ...'

'With sodding good cause.'

'... but no more sorry that I am.'

'Your kid isn't up the bleeding spout.'

'I have no children. That's a ridiculous remark to ...'

'But you're the bloody father.'

'I'm not denying that. I'm not ...'

'No. You'd better bloody-well not ...'

*'Will you stop swearing in this house!'*

Black blinked, as the sheer rage, riding the man's words, hit him. His nostrils quivered, the blood left his face, but he remained silent.

The man took a deep breath, before he spoke again.

He said, 'Mr Black, let me observe the obvious. She's little more than a child ... and I'm a grown man. There is no possibility whatever of us ever becoming man and wife.'

'My Alice wouldn't have ...?'

'Nor would I dream of ever gracing your daughter with my name,' snapped the man. 'Anything along those lines, you can forget.'

'You graced her with your bloody plonker ... didn't you?' snarled Black.

The man closed his eyes for a moment, clenched his teeth to hold himself in check, then walked to the sideboard and poured neat whisky into a glass. He made no offer of hospitality towards Black.

'Does she want the child?' he said, at last.

'What the hell do *you* think?'

'Unless she's changed her mind ...'

'She hasn't.'

'Which means one of two things.' The man gulped whisky. 'Adoption, which she won't hear of, or abortion. One, or the other.'

'She don't want it,' bawled Black. 'She don't want to have it, then give the little bleeder away ... she just don't *want* it.'

'Quite. Abortion.'

Black scowled, and said, 'I'm not too bloody keen on ...'

'For God's sake!' exploded the man. 'We are not talking about drinking gin till it just *happens*. Jumping from some sideboard, for hours on end. We're discussing a properly conducted termination of pregnancy.'

'Without fuss. That's the main thing ... without fuss.'

'You mean quietly?'

'I mean *bloody* quietly.'

'Privately?'

'And you footing the bill, mate.'

'I know.' The man nodded. 'Privately – secretly, if possible ... and at my expense. Does *that* satisfy you?'

Black sniffed, scowled his worry for a few moments then, eventually, growled, 'How the hell I'm gonna tell the father ...'

'*I'm* the father.' The man stared. 'I've already admitted ...'

'I mean the father – the *father* ... we're good Catholics, and when we tell the father he'll ...'

'I know exactly what he'll say,' groaned the man.

'Aye. So do I.'

The man finished the whisky in a single swallow, then said, 'That's something between you and him. Between you and your conscience. I can't advise you ... I'd be a fool to try. But, the pregnancy has to be terminated – and it *has*, regardless of any religious meddling – and I'm willing to foot the bill. Every penny. I've already made arrangements. That's why I invited you round. That's what I wanted to tell you. Personally. I didn't ask you here for a non-productive slanging match. Just to put all the cards on the table, and sort some way out of this infernal tragedy. That's all.'

A man – an educated man – wrestling with one of the problems of the permissive society. That's how *he* spent part of that evening.

It was an evening he could have done well without.

Quincey – Albert Quincey – spent a good percentage of that evening keeping an eye on Nic Emmerson.

These nig-nogs ... you never *knew*. They weren't like people. More like animals. And Emmerson was in a position where he could do the club a lot of no-good. Gas the drinks to hell. Short-change the customers. Get stroppy with some big-spender.

He could do the club some *real* no-good.

And Quincey knew why the old coon was worried. Exactly why. Quincey knew what was making him fumble the drinks and (on two occasions) let a very pricey glass slip from his fingers and smash itself to blazes on the floor, behind the bar-counter. This brown-faced nerk had worries on his shoulders; lots of worries ... and you could forget all that yes-sir-no-sir-three-bags-full-sir garbage about 'retiring'. This Uncle Sambo retiring? The day *he* retired, you could fry snowballs in deep fat, and serve 'em with chips.

Quincey *knew*.

Which was why, for much of that evening, Quincey hovered around the bar and watched Emmerson with suspicious eyes; waiting for the first real sign – waiting to see the topple start ... and then (by Christ!) he'd give the old thumbscrew a few extra turns.

Whereas, that same evening, Joyce – Randal Alexander Osbert Joyce – de-flowered a virgin and, surprising as it may sound, for the first time in his life.

It wasn't his first *time*, you understand ... not by a ball of string. But, until that time, he'd always followed somebody else. He'd never broken new territory. He'd always had full and active co-operation, because the bint had always known as many tricks as he'd known ... and, sometimes, *more*.

But, this time ...

'I'm – I'm ... I've never done this before.'

It hadn't been a refusal. Not even a token objection. If anything, it had been a stammered apology.

Then, shortly afterwards, she whispered, 'Please show me. Teach me. Anything!'

The pundits all insist that every man remembers his first woman; that no matter how many times he makes love – no matter how many times he fornicates – that first time is always special enough to stand like a diamond amidst a cluster of rubies.

Not so – not always so ... not (for example) with Detective Constable Joyce.

He turned away from her, to zip and belt his trousers – to grant her the privacy of pulling the old-fashioned cami-knickers into place and straightening her dress – and, at that moment, he felt something not too far removed from shame.

He mumbled, 'I'm – I'm – er ... y'know.'

'Yes?' Her voice was quiet and steady. 'You can turn round now, Mr Joyce.'

He turned, faced her then lowered his eyes.

'Yes?' she repeated.

'I – I shouldn't have . . .'

'Oh, but you *should*,' she said, softly. 'You've done nothing wrong, Mr Joyce. Nothing of which to be ashamed. Nothing I didn't *want* you to do.'

His mouth was dry – his voice had a croaking quality – as he said, 'Thank you. Thank you, for saying that.'

'No. It's I who should thank you.' As he looked up at her, her face flushed slightly, and she added, 'Tell me, truthfully. Was I . . . *adequate?*'

'You were beautiful,' he breathed.

'Oh, come now . . .'

'I swear.'

'It's nice of you to say so.' The smile had a sad, wistful overtone. 'Very gentlemanly.' The smile widened, and she asked, 'Now . . . more tea?'

'May I visit you again?' he asked, sombrely.

'No.' The smile stayed in place, but she shook her head. 'I've no desire to become your mistress, Mr Joyce.'

'No . . . I mean, to talk. To talk with you.'

'About what?'

'Anything. Everything.'

She touched the neck of her dress – the perfect, feminine gesture – as she said, 'I have a mother, Mr Joyce. I have a responsibility towards her . . . she's an old, and ailing, lady. This evening, for a few minutes, I deliberately ignored that responsibility. I didn't even *care*. But, it's the first time, and it has to be the last. As a member of the present-day generation, I don't expect you to understand . . . but it's my decision, and I made it many years ago.'

'Just to talk?' he pleaded, gently.

'No. Not even to talk . . . because, we both know that, after what's happened, we wouldn't be content with *talking*.'

She paused, returned the smile to her face, and ended, 'Now
... tea?'

All Joyce could say was, 'Please.'

She left for the kitchen, and Joyce lowered himself into
an armchair.

For the life of him, he couldn't understand why she
wouldn't believe – why, with her breathless desire to please,
with her controlled but passionate response to his every
caress, with her innocence of every artificial ploy, she
wouldn't believe – she still wouldn't believe him when he
spoke no less than the truth ... that, indeed, she *had* been
beautiful.

Bert Hicks spent the evening boozing ... then fighting.

Having picked up his car, he drove to Bordfield, parked
then wandered into *The Wounded Warrior* for an odd pint.
The odd one soon became the odd two ... soon became
the odd half-dozen ... soon became the odd lost count.

He used the tap-room, and in the tap-room there was a
dart board. The dart board was in use, all evening. Bert
Hicks didn't go for sissy games like darts but (as luck would
have it) his seat was alongside the board and, consequently,
within easy reach of the darts, as they thudded into the
board.

The general basis of the discussion was football but,
gradually, as the total consumption of beer mounted, the
generalities became less general and specifics entered the
argument. Specific matches, specific players, specific teams.

Leeds United.

The man who disagreed with Hicks instanced Leeds
United ... and Leeds United was Hicks's favourite team.

'Watch it,' growled Hicks.

'They're bloody dirty,' emphasised the man. 'When
they're winning ... okay. Then, they play a good game.

But, Jesus, let 'em look like coming off second-best ...
they're just plain *dirty*.'

At which point Hicks leaned across the table and planted
a fist on the man's mouth.

The man swore, stood up, grabbed a half-empty pint
tankard and ear-holed Hicks with it ... hard.

Hicks, too, stood up, closed his fist around two darts
which were embedded in the handy board, and drove the
points at his opponent's left eye ... *and* almost scored a
double-bull!

Ten minutes later, the cops arrived to collect the empties.

By ten-thirty, a hospital medic was explaining to the man
how near he'd been to a fifty-per-cent sight-loss, and a
police station desk sergeant was explaining to Hicks what
was meant by G.B.H., D. and D., and Conduct Likely
to cause a Breach of the Peace.

One more evening blooded itself and attained the stature of
night ... and, via its half-million component parts, the city
lived, breathed and pulsated.


10.55 pm ......


Nor was the twin city of Lessford one ounce less rum-
bustious, or one gramme less alive; it, too, greeted the night
with garish lights and raucous laughter – with loving and
fighting – with laughter and pontification ... with the whole
gamut of human emotion.

Except (as with Bordfield) on the fringes of the city; in
the posh districts, where indiscretions were no fewer, but
were conducted in a more civilised manner and, wherever

possible, were kept under well-lashed-down wraps.

There was (for example) this cul-de-sac ...

It was well beyond earshot of the noise and bustle of the city. It was tree-lined (rowans and planes), with ancient gas-lamps modified to accept the city's electric street-lighting, and the electrified gas-lamps were level with the swell of the tree branches, which meant that much of the illumination was shaded, and the cul-de-sac was a place of soft light, dappled with black shadows. The houses in this cul-de-sac were huge and monstrous; ugly edifices to Victorian affluence and bad taste. It was a strange place – a creepy place, at this o'clock – and a place unknown to the bulk of the citizens of Lessford.

The slim man, wearing the grey Homburg, the white scarf and the dark, belted overcoat, paid off the taxi at the mouth of the cul-de-sac. The second man (equally slim) watched from one of the darker shadows. The second man wore a leather wind-cheater, army-twill trousers and sneakers. He wore neither hat nor cap.

The taxi drove away, and the man with the grey Homburg walked briskly along the pavement, between the dappled light and shade.

The man in the wind-cheater eased himself farther into the darkness.

As the man in the Homburg passed, the man in the wind-cheater spoke. He spoke softly, and in a voice which carried only as far as the passing man; softly but clearly ... and as if repeating some regularly recited rote.

He said, 'Permission to test the guns, skipper?'

(......'Permission to test the guns, skipper?'
Flight Lieutenant Collins lifted a gloved hand from the control column, touched the switch on his oxygen-mask mike, and said, 'When you're ready, gunners.'

57

*Alf, from the mid-upper, and Ray, the bomb-aimer, from
the nose-turret, spoke together.*

*Alf said, 'Testing guns.'*

*Ray said, 'Thanks, skipper. Testing.'*

*Collins returned his hand to the control column. Through-
out the short exchange his eyes had never left the bank
of dimly-lit dials which stretched the width of the cabin.*

*Those dials – those quivering needles – they spoke their
own silent language. From the guts of the roaring Merlins.
From the fuel tanks and the air-speed indicator. From the
gyro-compass and the oil pipes. Dials, and quivering needles
– many of them in quadruplet – each glowing a ghostly,
green fluorescence in the darkness of the cabin.*

*And, beyond the cabin – out there, on the trailing edges
of the two great wings – the exhaust cowlings also glowed.
Bright orange, fading into dull red, with a stubby tail of
blue-hot exhaust gas.*

*Necessary – because those four Merlins were necessary,
to lift the Lancaster into the air, deliver the bomb-load
to the target, then race for home – but, nevertheless, a mite
hair-raising. A little like carrying four socking great Roman
candles with you, over enemy territory.*

*Not that they were visible, beyond a few hundred yards;
the boffins were quite adamant ... the exhausts couldn't be
seen from the ground. Collins believed the boffins, because
the boffins were paid to know these things, but ...*

*That little 'but' tended to bring on the muck-sweat.*

*In the blackness to starboard fireflies twinkled against
the night sky.*

*'Junior', the flight-engineer edged his way into the cabin,
plugged in his intercom, and said, 'Fuel tanks balanced
up, skipper.'*

*Collins nodded his understanding.*

*'Junior' eased himself into the second dickie seat, glanced*

through the perspex, saw the fireflies, and said, 'They've dropped an egg on Heligoland. We're on course ... more or less.'

Once more, Collins nodded without replying.

Odd, how predictable the Germans were. This – one of Five Group's regular ploys – sending the odd Lanc. over Heligoland, dropping a couple of bombs, to stir up the flack. Either Heligoland, or Dunkirk. Miles to one side of the main force, but within sight. And, with that sighting of flack everybody could get a bearing, and the ropey navigators could rectify their courses and speeds.

And the Germans obliged ... always!

One of the many tricks of this particularly suicidal trade. One of the thousand and one tiny ways of tilting the balance, ever so slightly, and making it possible to invade enemy airspace, surrounded by ear-splitting noise – blind, and trusting in the skill of instrument-makers and the cunning of your own navigator – to deliver canned explosive, to dodge the searchlights and the anti-aircraft fire, to outwit the nightfighters ... and (hopefully) return to enjoy the luxury of a fried egg.

Thanks, in small part, to Heligoland – or Dunkirk – and the predictability of the Germans.

The Lancaster shuddered, as if shouldering its way through a particularly solid piece of air, and Collins's gloved hands tightened on the control column.

Over the intercom, the voice of John, the navigator, said, 'Jerryland coming up, skipper.'

'Mid-upper okay.'

'Front turret okay.'

Collins flicked his mike switch, and said, 'Jim?'

From the rear turret, the gunner's voice said, 'I'll castrate that bloody armourer. This top, left-hand gun. I told him it was tending to jam.'

'*Fire, and re-cock,*' *intoned Alf's voice.*

'*Quiet,*' *said Collins. Then, to the rear-gunner, '*Can you clear it, Jim?*'*

'*Yeah, I can clear it. But it jams again, every sixth or seventh round.*'

'*The other three?*'

'*They're okay. Just the top, left-hand ... it jams every sixth or seventh round.*'

*Alf said, '*It sounds like the servo-feed.*'*

'*Yeah. Could be.*'

*Collins said, '*Clear it, and cock it, Jim. Then leave it ... and hope.*'*

'*Okay, skipper.*'

*Collins took his eyes from the dials long enough to glance out of the cabin and find the thread of surf which sent faint reflection back from ten-thousand feet below.*

*He said, '*Stand by, gunners. Stand by, crew. No more unnecessary talk. We're crossing the coast. We're starting the search-roll, now.*')*

Externally, the house was an abomination. Internally, the ground-floor flat showed nothing but restrained elegance.

The near-museum-piece furniture had been designed for a room such as the large, high-ceilinged main room. The matching, high-backed, wing-chairs; brass-studded and up-holstered in ox-blood leather. And, between the chairs, the brass-bound, military chest whose polished surface did per-fect duty as a coffee-table. The settle, against one of the walls; a thing of delicacy and green baize; of minute inlay and surprising hidden strength.

The room was furnished with such pieces. Not too many, and all there to be used.

'Nice.' Crowe turned his head, slowly, and murmured, 'Ve-ery nice, skip.'

60

'I like it,' smiled Collins. He peeled off hat, coat and scarf and tossed them onto the settle. 'Now, James, coffee? Or would you prefer something stronger?'

'Coffee's fine.'

'Please make yourself comfortable. I won't be a minute.'

Collins left the main room of the flat, and Crowe strolled to one of the walls to scrutinise four, first-class Dürer reproductions: *A Hare, Study of the Head of an Old Man, Study of Plants* and *Study of Hands in Adoration.*

'The detail,' said Collins, as he returned. He was carrying a large, silver charger upon which were stacked crockery, sugar-bowl, cream-jug and a man-sized Thermos jar. As he placed the charger on the military-chest coffee-table, he continued, 'Dürer missed nothing. The curls in that old man's beard ... he's captured every hair. And the eyes ... downcast, and with just the right amount of resigned bitterness.'

'I go for the hare,' observed Crowe.

'Someone else did,' said Collins, softly.

'Eh?'

'You didn't know him. He's dead.'

'Oh!'

Crowe left the pictures and settled himself in one of the wing-chairs.

Collins poured steaming coffee from the Thermos jar.

Crowe said, 'A bachelor's trick.'

'The Thermos?'

'Cheaper than a wife ... and just as effective.'

'As far as coffee's concerned,' agreed Collins.

'Uhuh.'

'As you say, a bachelor's trick.' Collins sat down in the other wing-chair, and they each spooned sugar into the poured coffee. Neither of them used the cream. 'Whenever I have an evening on the town, I do it. It's pleasant to know there's a hot drink waiting.'

'An evening on the town?' The grin exposed teeth, as white and as even as the keys of a new Steinway.

'The Amadeus String Quartet.' Collins's returned smile balanced the extrovert grin of Crowe. 'They don't visit Lessford very often.'

'A real hot gig,' chuckled Crowe.

'Haydn's Quartet in E flat major, and Brahms's Quartet in C minor ... among others.'

'Yeah – like I say ... a real swinging session.'

Collins's smile widened and, for a few moments, they sipped coffee in silence.

Then, Crowe said, 'You ain't asked me, skipper.'

'What?'

'What brought me here.'

'I take it for granted. You were visiting Lessford, and decided to look me up ... you don't need an excuse, James. Any of you. Any of the old crew. But, unfortunately, we've lost touch ... despite all the promises we made. It always happens, I'm afraid. Life goes on. We lose touch.'

'Not me.'

'No? Tell me.'

'Okay.' Crowe leaned forward, fractionally, in his chair, and said, 'Let's start with Ray, the bomb-aimer. He's back in New Zealand. In banking. Married – a coupla kids ... maybe three grandchildren, by this time. Last I heard, he had two. Up to last year, he was no small cog in the Barclays Group ... at four rue Esprit-des-Lois at Bordeaux. Then he got this New Zealand offer – back home – and took it.

' "Junior" ... would you believe "Junior's" on an oil-rig? The guy who used to nurse the juice, like it was liquid gold. Now, he's on a North Sea gusher. Married – no kids

... his home-base is Aberdeen. He's making bread, like you wouldn't believe.

'Johnny, the navigator ... he ain't with us, any more.'

'I'm sorry,' murmured Collins.

'I don't think *he* was, skip,' said Crowe. 'I heard. I visited him, about a month before the end. The old steel crab – lung cancer ... man, did he look rough! He left a widow and a kid. A daughter. She's married to a nice guy, in local government – Manchester way ... they're looking after Johnny's widow, good.

'Alfie – the mid-upper ... remember Alfie?'

'Of course.'

'That guy ... could he talk? Still can. He's in insurance. Started at the ground floor, and worked like a dog. He's on the board of directors ... that's how hard he's worked. I see him, pretty often. He throws a little pay-dirt in my direction, whenever he can.'

'And your job?' asked Collins.

'Oh, I just horse around,' fenced Crowe. 'Remember Mac ... the wireless-op?'

'Of course.'

'He hit the rocks.' Crowe frowned his concern. 'He moved in with bad company. About two years after the war. Divorced. Right now, he's serving his second term behind the wall.'

'Good lord! I'm sorry to hear that.'

'Yeah. I'm sorry to have to tell you, skip. I've seen him a coupla times – visiting days ... you wouldn't know him. He's gone crook. Real *crook*.'

'That's pretty terrible,' sighed Collins.

'Yeah.'

Collins sipped at his coffee then, in a nostalgic tone, said, 'We were a good crew, James. A lucky crew.'

'We'd a good skipper.'

'Moderately ... no more than that.'

'Okay – a *lucky* skipper ... that was even more important. Lucky enough to take us through two tours, and a bit.'

'Seventy-two times,' mused Collins, and shook his head in wonderment.

Crowe gave a twisted grin, and said, 'Seventy-two times – and shit-scared every time ... *me*, at any rate.'

'All of us.'

'Young, and bloody mad.'

'You've kept track,' said Collins. 'That's more than I have.'

'An exercise,' said Crowe, off-handedly.

Collins smiled his curiosity, and said, 'And the pilot?'

'Yeah ... you, too.' Crowe grinned a little self-consciously. 'Remember? You wanted to be a barrister?'

'I did, indeed.'

'My griff says things went wrong, and you settled for being a cop.'

Collins nodded, and the nod was touched with regret.

'But, a good cop,' continued Crowe. 'I'd even say a fine cop ... a cop who earned his chief-superintendentship, and his retirement.'

'It was a good second-best,' admitted Collins.

'I have other griff, too,' said Crowe, softly. He paused, then continued, 'It says that you fixed a certain bastard called Gunter. Paul Gunter. He had it coming ... up to, and including, the orange-crate. My griff says you fixed its delivery, skip ... and, since you retired.'*

Collins leaned forward in his chair, and topped up both cups with coffee from the Thermos jug.

'You seem to be well informed, James,' he drawled.

'Yeah. I keep my ear close to the ground.'

* See *Death of a Big Man*

'I also have the impression that this is *not* – strictly speaking – a social visit.'

'It's nice to see you, skip.'

'It's nice to see *you*, James ... but that doesn't answer my question.'

Crowe added more sugar to the topped-up coffee, and said, 'Answer me a question, will you, skipper?'

'No promises, James. That depends on the question.'

'Remember Operational Training Unit?'

Collins nodded.

'The tea-and-wad waggon ... when we all had a fortnight to sort ourselves into crews?'

Collins said, 'As I recall – that tea-and-wad waggon – it was while we were waiting to be served that I asked you to join my crew.'

'Yeah.' Crowe pinched his nose, then said, 'You never told me why.'

'Let's say – in naval jargon – I liked the cut of your jib.'

'Yeah ... then, let's say horse feathers. I wasn't the best gunner there. Not at that time. I learned fast – maybe because you'd picked me ... but, at that time, I was a poor bet.'

'I picked you,' said Collins, quietly and without emotion, 'because I liked the look of you. That's the only reason.'

'And that's the *only* reason?'

Collins's eyes twinkled with gentle mischief, as he said, 'It was going to be night-flying ... mostly. It seemed to me that, with your complexion, you'd be less likely to be seen.'

'Skipper, I love you.' Crowe's face split into a grin of sheer delight. 'You have a great way of calling a spade a spade.'

Garfield watched the sleeping youth, and worried.

Where the hell was Hicks?

The world – Garfield's world, and the world in general – might spin that little more smoothly if all the Hickses in creation had never been conceived, but the Hickses were around ... and, in a situation like this, the Hickses were handy. Not, strictly speaking, necessary. But, nevertheless, handy.

Take Pete, here ...

Okay – it wasn't kidnapping ... it really wasn't *kidnapping*. But, sure as hell, that's what the cops were going to *call* it, if things came unstitched. The cops weren't going to believe the truth; that it was all a very involved bluff; that, if they could have grabbed the money, without touching Pete – without even scaring Pete's father – that's the way they'd have done it. Taking Pete was a gag. Bringing him here, to this lousy farmhouse, was a gag. Fastening him to the bed, with the leg-iron, was a gag. It was all one big, involved gag, with a thirty-thousand-quid punch line.

Al had said so. Al had stressed that fact, and Garfield had believed him ... otherwise Garfield wouldn't have touched the job. Hicks had believed him – or, at least, Garfield hoped Hicks had believed him ... but, with a lout like Hicks, who could be sure.

And now this ... where the hell was Hicks?

The man behind the eight-ball. His name wasn't Hicks. *His* name was Leonard Garfield ... thank you very much! Sucker Number One, as usual. And, supposing old man

66

Emmerson ran to the cops, Sucker Number One was going to be a very much wanted man. Because he'd been driving the taxi. And, because – and in front of the middle-aged dame who'd brought him out of the school building – Pete, here, had named names. And the name he'd named had been 'Mr Garfield'.

And now (for God's sake!) Pete was asleep.

No panic. No sweat. This fifteen-year-old coloured kid was behaving as if being snatched was as common, and as painless, as having a hair-cut. Okay ... maybe he knew. Maybe he realised ... that nobody was going to *hurt* him, anyway. That it was all a gag. A come-on, to get some easy bread, and enough bread to make the come-on worth while. Maybe ...

Maybe anything ... *but where the hell was Hicks?*

He looked at the youth, sleeping peacefully under the patchwork-squared quilt. For a moment, his nostrils flared as a tiny burst of anger for the injustices of life touched his mind. Then he smiled and spoke soft words of self-pity.

He said, 'Just to be your age again, kid. To know the answers – the answers I *now* know ... and to be your age, again.'

'You weren't as bad, in those days,' observed Collins.

Crowe said, 'Could be I was a little scared, skip.'

'You weren't as bad,' insisted Collins. 'It meant a lot less.'

'Let's say I've learned how much it *really* means.'

They'd finish the coffee. Collins had switched on two bars of an attractive electric fire, to add more warmth to that supplied by the central-heating radiators. One corner of the huge room was taken up by a floor-to-ceiling assemblage of the only hobby Collins allowed himself – the wherewithal via which he could enjoy good music – and the hi-fi, stereo record-player-cum-radio-cum-cassette-player-cum-cartridge-player-cum-tape-recorder was tastefully encased in purpose-built cupboards and shelves which (via some mystic trick of sheer craftsmanship) blended with, and even augmented, the beauty of the room's near-antique furniture. The strategically placed twin speakers were turned low – low enough not to interfere with the conversation, but high enough to fill the spaces of silence with pleasant sound – and, as a background to their talk, the baroque music of Gabrieli seemed to bespatter their words with soft, but beautiful, punctuation.

They each leaned back and luxuriated in the comfort of the wing-chairs. They both smoked cigarettes; Collins smoking his in a four-inch-long briar holder.

They were friends – old friends, and firm friends – but friends who had been parted for too long, and they each used words and phrases as probes in their search for some communal base upon which they could build the necessary bridge with which to span then and now.

Crowe said, 'Don't get me wrong, skip. Not you. But, there aren't many like you.'

'You, too, had dreams, James ... as I recall. I wanted to be a barrister. You were keen to become a social worker.'

'Dreams. You know all about dreams, skipper. Yours didn't come true, either.'

'And yours?' asked Collins, gently.

'What do you think?'

'I think you'd have made an excellent social worker ... since you ask.'

'Skipper!' Crowe drew hard on the cigarette then, as if itemising certain facts, for his own benefit, continued, 'Full-blooded Jamaican ... that's me. British born, but only just. My folks came from Kingston. Kingston folk ... coming to the Home Country. To Tiger Bay, of all places. And that's

68

where I was born ... within three months of their arrival.

'Okay, they panned the hell outa me, but made me stay good. What the other kids did didn't matter. Jimmy Crowe was gonna be a good boy. A good citizen ... with some sorta education. That much they did. That much they gave me. That, and pride.

'It sticks, skipper. That pride ... it really sticks. It made me volunteer for air-crew. One of the good things it did ... it made me meet you. And the other guys. We were a good bunch. Flying apart, we were still a good bunch. Buddies. Y'know ... I sometimes think. From Jamaica – from New Zealand – from all parts of the U.K. ... and we *still* made a great team. On ops. In, or out, of those bloody Lancs ... we *still* made a great team.'

'The dream of being a social worker?' Collins reminded him quietly.

'It turned sour.'

'Why?'

'Why the hell not?'

'Or, did *you* turn sour, James? Is that the reason?'

'Part, I guess. *It* turned sour – *I* turned sour ... two sours don't make a sweet taste, either way.'

'Specifically?' insisted Collins.

'We-ell, I'll tell you.' Once more Crowe drew cigarette smoke deep into his lungs. 'The names ... see? Nig-nog. Wog. Nigger ... that ain't used too often, these days, but it *was*. A man gets tired of it, in time. That's what I am, skipper – a man ... a fully-paid-up member of the human race. And, some of the bastards who don't think so, I wouldn't waste spit on.'

'That's why they don't think so,' said Collins, with a smile.

'Yeah ... I guess.'

'So-o, chip-on-the-shoulder Crowe couldn't make it?'

There was gentle mockery in the question; the mockery reserved for true friendship.

'Could be,' sighed Crowe.

'You've disappointed me, James.'

'Yeah.' Crowe smiled. 'Maybe I could say the same, skip. You ain't a barrister ... Maybe *you've* disappointed *me*.'

The Gabrieli piece ended, there was a second or two of silence, then the music of Vivaldi picked up the musical baton.

'So, what are you?' asked Collins.

'Uh?'

'As one failure to another – as a barrister who didn't make it, to a social worker who didn't make it – what's your profession, James?'

Crowe chuckled quietly, then said, 'Like you, skip. Un-skilled labour. I'm a cop ... of sorts. One-man investigation agency.'

'A private detective!' Collins sounded almost shocked.

'A shamus.'

'Good God!'

'It's a living,' said Crowe. 'And I don't touch divorce ... so it ain't a cut-glass-and-caviare living.'


11.25 pm ......


Bert Hicks wasn't quite as drunk as he had been. He was still a little drunk – drunk enough to take stupid risks, and drunk enough to think he could chew iron filings and spit barbed wire – but sober enough to know that a police cell was a place from which he should absent himself, as soon

70

as possible. In short, he was dangerously drunk ... and drunk enough to get away with things.

The constable doing all-night desk duty, on the other hand, was stone cold sober ... but tired, and bored to hell. He was a middle-aged cop who, instead of catching up with sleep (which was his normal way of spending a portion of daylight hours, when on night-shift), had, instead, driven thirty miles to attend the wedding of a niece, then driven thirty miles back. Thus, he was tired. He was bored, because it was a quiet night and (at this moment) the night duty sergeant was out on the streets, checking that the beat boys were busy pounding holes in pavements ... therefore, he had nobody with whom to talk, or argue, or generally use as a means of shifting the sand from under his eyelids.

Indeed, the buzz from the cell area was something he almost welcomed as a small relief from the bone-weary monotony.

He began a sigh, which changed its mind, midway, and ended as a stifled yawn, unhooked the keys from the Charge Office cabinet, and slowly made his way to the cells.

At Number Three Cell, he opened the Judas window, bent his head to peer inside, and said, 'What's up, now?'

Hicks was sprawling on the composition floor of the cell.

'Hicks!' called the cop.

Hicks neither answered nor moved.

'Hicks!' bawled the cop a second time and, when the sprawling figure still didn't move, added a muttered, 'Oh, my Christ ... what *now*?' unlocked the cell door and entered the cell to investigate.

He bent over Hicks, rolled him onto his back and, in that hair-line breadth of a second, before Hicks's finger found his throat, realised he'd fallen for a trick as old as Eve's apple-gag.

The struggle didn't last long. Less than a minute. The

cop was past the blood-and-snot stage of his career, and his staff was upstairs in the drawer of a Charge Office desk. He tried for a knee in Hicks's groin, but Hicks sensed its coming and rolled clear and, gradually, the cop's face turned scarlet, then puce – his eyes popped, and his mouth opened, and his jaw quivered – then, the blackness came.

Hicks drove his fingers home, and held them there far longer than was necessary.

A cop, who was not particularly dumb – merely human, humane and tired, after a long day without sleep – died, and Hicks made his cautious way from an empty police station and into the freedom of the streets.

'The coloureds don't trust the fuzz,' said Crowe, bluntly.

'Why? Policemen – most policemen – are colour-blind, in that respect.'

'That's what you say, skip.'

'And, James – as an educated man – that's what you *know*.'

It wasn't an argument. It wasn't really a difference of opinion ... it was merely a statement of unpalatable truths, as expressed from differing viewpoints.

They were still smoking cigarettes – their third, or fourth, by this time – and, instead of coffee, they were sipping medium dry Amontillado sherry. The twin speakers still provided baroque background to their talk; Vivaldi had given way to Bach, and now Bach was giving way to Corelli.

Crowe said, 'Skipper – maybe *I* know it ... but they don't. And they ain't readily convinced. I work from Liverpool ... and *there's* a place. Coloureds. Roman Catholics. Protestants. Even the Welsh and the Irish. They don't trust each other ... and *none* of 'em trust the cops. Ain't that something? Don't that make crime detection a sick joke?'

72

'And you?' asked Collins, suavely. 'Do they trust you?'

'The skin helps,' admitted Crowe.

'Meaning you work with the police?'

'Oh, no.' Crowe shook his head, sadly. 'I'm private ... strictly private. Alfie – I've already said – he throws the occasional bone in my direction. Some insurance enquiry. Some jerk who figures he can beat the system. That pays pretty good money. But – this is gonna stick in your craw, skip – lots of the folks come to my place, *instead* of going to the cops. I'm one of them ... that's the way they see things.'

'Crime enquiries?' There was censure in the question.

'Uhuh.' Crowe shook his head, slowly. 'They come for advice. I nose around a little. Get the thing off the ground, maybe. Then, I tell 'em. I don't mince words. The fuzz. They take what they know – what I've dug up for 'em ... and they tell some guy who carries enough authority to help. And they keep my name outa things.'

'It's one way,' said Collins wrily.

'What?'

'Social work. Breaking down barriers, between the public and the police.'

'Yeah ... could be.'

There was a silence. This time, it was a prolonged silence. It lasted all of three minutes. The baroque music danced, in the silence, like audible pollen being shaken from the anthers of tiny but beautiful flowers. They moistened their lips with Amontillado, and dragged soothing cigarette smoke into their lungs.

And they waited – each for the other ... because they both knew that the small-talk had been exhausted. The touching, and groping, and feeling-out was all finished. The only subject left was the reason for Crowe's visit.

73

Very carefully, Crowe said, 'You ain't a gambling man, skipper. You *weren't*. That still so?'

'I don't gamble,' admitted Collins, quietly.

'Not even a flutter? The National? The Derby?'

'No ... not even a flutter.'

'Football pools?' asked Crowe, innocently.

'I wouldn't know how to fill in a coupon. Football isn't my game.'

'Yeah. But supposing ...'

'What?'

'Just – y'know ... *supposing*.'

'What, exactly, am I expected to suppose?'

'Football pools,' said Crowe. 'The only way some poor guys are ever likely to hit real money.'

'The odds are very much against it.'

'They try,' insisted Crowe. 'The only odds they have in life. So they try. And, sometimes – *sometimes* – it happens.'

'Sometimes,' agreed Collins.

'Okay – supposing it was you. Supposing you'd put a cross in the little square.'

'Which little square?'

'The one on the coupon. The one you put a cross in, if you don't want publicity ... don't want the world to know you've won big money.'

'I'm sorry. I didn't know.'

'The pools people don't like it too much. They like the publicity.'

'Naturally.'

'But – it's part of the agreement – a cross in the square means no publicity ... and a lot of dough *has* been paid out to folks the rest of the world don't know.'

'Really? You surprise me.'

'You still "supposing", skipper?' asked Crowe, softly.

'Of course. If you insist.'

'Okay. You fill in the pools. You've been filling 'em in for years. Then, one week, you hit the jackpot. Thirty-two-thousand ... a little over. And no publicity.'

'It's rather a staggering thought,' murmured Collins.

'Yeah ... especially if you're poor black.'

'Ah!' breathed Collins.

'What's that mean, skipper?'

'You tell *me*, James. I have the distinct feeling that you're trying to find a way to tell me *something*.'

In a dreamy, slow-speaking voice, Crowe said, 'Thirty-two G. And a boy ... a fifteen-year-old kid. And a widower. And coloured. That's a great combination, skip.'

Collins made a soft, 'Mmmm,' sound.

'For a snatch, I mean,' ended Crowe, without a change of tone.

'Kidnapping?' Collins spoke the word quite distinctly, and it dropped like a stone, down a deep well.

'For thirty of the thirty-two ... they ain't greedy, skipper. They're leaving him two grand. Ain't that generous of 'em?'

The Corelli piece ended and, after a few moments of silence, Vivaldi waltzed out of the twin speakers once more.

'I like this music,' said Collins, sombrely, 'but if you find it annoying ...'

'No – that's okay ... it's nice.'

'Soothing.'

'Yeah ... soothing.'

Collins rested an elbow on the arm of the wing-chair and held his sherry steady. He leaned back into the soft leather, and closed his eyes, as if concentrating all his attention upon the intricate weave of the music.

'Well?' asked Crowe.

Without opening his eyes, Collins drawled, 'A hypothetical question, James. An extremely hypothetical ques-

75

tion. I don't gamble ... therefore, I'm unlikely to win such a sum of money. I'm not married ... therefore, I haven't a son, and I certainly can't become a widower. And I'm not a coloured man. James – believe me – that's far too hypothetical a question for me to even contemplate.'

'You're not dumb, skipper,' said Crowe, flatly.

Still with his eyes closed, Collins said, 'And you don't trust me ... not completely.'

'You'd tell the guy to go to the cops ... right?'

'Excellent advice.'

'But, he don't trust the cops. He's coloured ... remember?'

'I remember.'

'And the word from the snatch-crowd is that the kid gets slaughtered, if he breathes a word to the cops.'

'Of course. That's a standard threat.'

'Skipper.' For the first time, urgency entered Crowe's voice. 'I need help. Somebody's help ... *your* help. This kid's my nephew. His father married my kid sister. She's dead ... but the old man loves him, like he was mother and father combined. He'll pay. Sure, he'll pay. But that's no guarantee. The kid could still get the chop.'

'Unfortunately,' murmured Collins.

'Judas Christ!' exploded Crowe. 'He's gonna pay. He's gonna throw his whole future down the nearest drain. He ain't gonna tell the cops ... and, for what? To be told where he can find his son's body? That's about the size of it, man. That's how these bastards operate ... supposing you don't know.'

'I know.' Collins moved his head in a tiny nod.

'And you ain't gonna do a thing. Not one damn thing. I come here, so sure – so damn sure – and ...'

'I'm proud you're so sure. I'm honoured, James.' Collins opened his eyes, rolled his head, looked at the coloured man, and smiled as he said, 'I only hope I don't let you down.'


11.45 pm ......


Garfield dozed in a particularly uncomfortable armchair, alongside the bed. It was an old armchair – soiled, and with its upholstery worn and, in places, ripped – with stuffing showing like grey pus, here and there – with springs which were tired and broken by misuse ... a *particularly* uncomfortable chair.

Nevertheless, Garfield cat-napped and, each time his mind wandered from the moorings of consciousness, it sailed a sea of dreams.

To beat the establishment ... to smash 'them' into a state of unconditional surrender ... to destroy and, after total destruction, to re-create.

Not as a Communist. Not as a Marxist. Not as an Anarchist. But as a free-thinker; as a believer in beauty, and the right to live your own life, without the restrictive humbug demanded by so-called 'civilisation'. To breathe pollution-free air. To drink pure water. To eat food not contaminated by chemicals.

That was part of it ... but there was much more.

Freedom, if it meant anything, meant complete freedom. The freedom from a man-made system of fisc; a return to barter or, at least, a realisation that metal counters and expensively-printed pieces of paper were not, of themselves, wealth; that the only real wealth was the wealth of life, itself, the wealth of the earth and the wealth of the produce of the earth, and that every living creature, from the moment of its

77

birth, was entitled, as of right, to its share of that wealth.

Freedom to go, or freedom not to go – freedom of choice
... and without boundaries, or passports, or airline tickets,
or *anything*.

Freedom from harassment – from the cops, from the
terrorists, from the war-mongers, from the killers ... freedom to live without fear.

Freedom to build ... not motor cars, not oil-tankers, not
roads or bridges, not high-rise flats or office-blocks. But,
freedom to *build*. Anything! Anywhere! To start with
virgin soil and, from that soil, construct Utopia ... and without having to crawl, cap in hand, for planning permission.

To build (among other things) a generation. A generation without cant, or humbug. A generation geared to worship the truth, and only the truth. A generation, of which
it might be said ... *this* is the reason, and the justification.
The whole evolution of man – the whole billion-year history
of the world itself – was for *this*.

Perfection!

Oh, for such a world ... Oh, for such a dream world ...
Oh, for such an impossible world. A world for the Gods, but
a world peopled by men. A world, complete and whole,
within the minds of the Garfields of the real world ... a
dreamer's world, destined for destruction via the harsh
truths of a world of reality.

And yet, despite the discomfort of the chair, Garfield
was happy ... for a few, glorious moments, he was *there*.

In his own perfect, but impossible, world.


Hicks's world, on the other hand, was a very frightening
world.

Hicks was suddenly as sober as the proverbial judge ...
and, be it understood, Hicks had had personal experience
concerning the soberness of *those* particular gentlemen.

To kill a copper. More than that, to kill him within the sanctity of his own nick. Jesus! It was like jumping from the top of the Post Office Tower and expecting to end up with nothing worse than a ricked ankle.

Hicks hardly dare breathe, in case he disturbed the atmosphere and brought his presence to the attention of every flatfoot in the city. He felt as if he was drowning in his own sweat; as if his heart had slipped its cable and was choking him; as if every tiny nerve-end under the surface of his skin had developed its own individual twitch.

Steaming Christ! ... *to kill a copper.*

He moved with infinite care. He peeped around every corner – he damn near peeped around every *brick* – before he edged himself from shadow to shadow ... to where?

To some stone, somewhere. To some hole in the ground. To some deep and unknown sewer. Anywhere ... just as long as it was somewhere the cops didn't know existed.

He tried to think.

Where the hell? Where the starving, stinking, screaming, howling *hell?*

He was up to the eyeballs in a snatch racket. He'd lumbered himself with a G.B.H. whack. And now, he'd ...

Ah!

The brainwave hit him, like a boulder at the back of the neck. The only place. The *obvious* place. The one place on God's earth where he'd be protected from the horrible vengeance of large men whose sole aim in life was going to be geared to belting ten shades of blue shit out of the unhappy, misguided berk who'd *had* to strangle one of their colleagues.

Safety ... if only he could make it.


Collins stood up from his chair, walked to the hi-fi equipment and killed the baroque background. It was, in a very obvious way, a gesture ... a 'coming on duty'. He squashed

79

his cigarette into an onyx ash-tray, remained standing, planted his feet firmly on the hearthrug, in front of the electric fire and, from there, fired pertinent questions at Crowe.

'This brother-in-law of yours. What's his name?'

'Emmerson. Nathaniel Emmerson ... but he usually answers to Nic.'

'Address?'

'Look, skipper, before I give you that, I need to know ...'

'I've no intention of notifying the police,' said Collins, irritably. 'Now – I'm sorry, James – but either trust me, or get out of here.'

'That's my old skipper,' grinned Crowe.

'His address?'

'Bordfield ... forty-seven Christopher Crescent.'

'That's not my old territory, James.'

'I know. It ain't *mine* ... I just blew in from Liverpool. But what's territory, when a kid's life's in hock?'

'Quite. By the way, what's the boy's name?'

'Peter.'

'And his age?'

'Fifteen ... going on sixteen.'

'Which means ...' A vertical furrow creased the skin between Collins's eyebrows. 'Let's be a little optimistic, James. Let's assume this nephew of yours is adult enough to be afraid, but not foolhardy.'

'He's a gutsy kid.'

'All right ... adult enough not to show his fear.'

'Yeah. He has that much.'

'Can we assume that he's not likely to act like some strip-cartoon character – Superman, or what have you – and try to fight his way out of wherever he is?'

'You can assume,' said Crowe, grimly, 'that if they've even mussed his goddam hair, they ain't gonna stand trial

80

'... not unless they have Crown Courts in hell.'

Collins cleared his throat, and murmured, 'Off the boil, James, if you please. A good fighter *never* loses his temper.'

Crowe took a deep breath, exhaled slowly, then nodded.

'Where did they pick him up?' asked Collins.

'At his school.'

'When?'

'This morning ... around noon, sometime. Before thirty-after.'

'You can't be more precise?'

'They phoned Nic at half-past noon. They had him, by that time.'

'They telephoned?'

'Yeah ... a greengrocer's shop, near Nic's place. Nic doesn't run to a phone.'

'And the message?'

'The usual crap. Thirty-thousand ... or else. And stay clear of the cops.'

'The exact words?'

'I dunno. I ain't seen Nic, yet.'

'Really?' Collins raised surprised brows.

'He phoned me. Just after three ...'

'From the greengrocer's shop?'

'No. From here ... from Lessford. He's scared stupid.'

'Too frightened to meet you?'

'Maybe.'

'He has to *be* seen. You realise that?'

'Yeah ... I guess.'

'Therefore, why not go to him, first – before coming here? Why not ...'

'Skipper, I ain't no miracle-man. Nic ... he thinks I am, see? But, I *know*. I'm a cheapskate, when it comes to a thing this size. I tool around on small stuff. This league? You want it straight, skip? I'm damn near as scared as Nic.

81

I could do something so bloody *stupid* ... and not even know.'

'All right.' Collins moved to the military-chest table. Helped himself to a cigarette and fitted it into the holder as he talked. 'The business of "no publicity". It's a comparative thing, of course.'

'Uh?'

'It's not completely confidential. It can't be.'

'We-ell, I dunno. You put a cross in the box, and ...'

'*Somebody* has to know,' said Collins impatiently. 'Use your head, James. The people who run the football pool, they must ...'

'Oh, Jesus!'

'What?'

'How in hell do we wade our way through *them*?'

'We don't.' Collins snapped a lighter, and touched the end of the cigarette with the flame. 'We can – at this point – take certain things for granted. That certain improbable things have not happened. That – for example – the Post Office have *not* opened your brother-in-law's mail, and thus broken this seal of confidentiality. That the men and women employed by the football pool organisation are to be trusted. The only way to tackle this thing, with any hope of success, is to start at the other end. At the small end. With your brother-in-law.'

'I don't think Nic ...'

'He told *somebody*.'

'I dunno,' said Crowe, doubtfully. 'He ain't likely to ...'

'He told you.'

'Yeah. But ...'

'We can presume he told his son.'

'Sure, but ...'

'You – in turn – have told me.'

'Look, skipper ...'

'It's a fairly safe bet that his son mentioned the win to some other person he thought he could trust. And your brother-in-law. And the people *they* told.'

'For God's sake!'

'What I'm getting at,' smiled Collins, 'is that there are very few secrets in this world. *Very* few. Remember the old days? Remember the war? Remember how many times they *knew* we were coming – almost before we did – and the reception committees they had waiting for us?'

'Do I not,' growled Crowe. 'As if anybody could ever forget.'

'And those,' said Collins, softly, 'were official, and very closely guarded, secrets. Secrecy. Confidentiality.' Collins shook his head. 'If those two words meant *anything*, no crime would ever be detected.'

'So-o?' sighed Crowe.

'We sit things out. We sweat it out, until morning. We have patience. Enough patience to wait for the kidnappers to make their various moves ... and, eventually, their *wrong* move.'

'I'm scared, skip,' muttered Crowe.

'*They're* scared,' countered Collins. 'That's one of our trump cards. That they're more scared than we are. The delicacy of play demands that we make sure they remain scared ... but, at the same time, not scared enough to kill the boy, as a means of covering their tracks, before they have the ransom money.'

'Yeah ... I guess. But, Christ, it's like juggling with razors.'

'It's been done,' said Collins, soothingly. 'It can be done again.' In a more brisk tone, he added, 'You'll stay here the night, of course.'

'Uhuh.' Crowe shook his head. 'I'm booked in at a transport kip.'

83

'There's a bed, already made. You're more than welcome, James.'

'Thanks, skipper.' Crowe stood up. 'But – y'know ... the bed-and-breakfast caper might attract less attention. This gear ...' He motioned towards the wind-cheater. 'It ain't actually a disguise, but it ain't quite "at home" in a nice place like this.'

'You're very welcome,' repeated Collins.

'Yeah. I know – and it makes me feel good ... and that ain't bull. I figure I'll be up, and around Bordfield way, come morning. I'll contact Nic, and get the full gen ... then, I'll be in touch.'

Collins nodded his understanding.

They walked to the door of the flat and, as they parted, they shook hands. The grip of the white hand was as firm, and as friendly, as the grip of the black. The handshake meant something ... among other things, it meant that, whoever had kidnapped the youth, Peter Emmerson, were (albeit unknowingly) up against a very unique, and very deadly, combination.

# TUESDAY – OCTOBER 27th

1.45 am ......

This man ...

There are men (and some women) of whom it might be said that nature has indulged in a seaside-postcard-style joke. They are near-mutations of the human race. Their guts stick out, like beer casks. Their backsides are like twin, overstuffed pillows. Their shape is such that they waddle, rather than walk. The men, invariably, have billiard-ball-smooth skulls, apple-round cheeks, silly little snub noses and ridiculous Cupid-bow lips ... and all this atop a neck which resembles nothing so much as a pile of particularly thick pancakes, topped off by blancmange jowls.

This man was one such man. He was a walking giggle – a perambulating guffaw ... but (as with many such men) innocently unaware of the fact.

He saw nothing ludicrous, or even eccentric, in the wearing of a flannel nightshirt. Or the wearing of woollen bedsocks. Or, come to that, the quartet of cats which crawled from under the covers as he heaved himself from the bed and lumbered across the room to answer the telephone.

He lifted the receiver from its rest, yawned, then said, 'Lennox.'

And then, what remained of his sleep left him. Like the dimming of the house-lights, the sudden beam of the limes and the raising of the curtain to reveal a brilliantly illuminated stage, he became fully awake.

85

He said, 'Don't touch a thing, inspector. Notify Mr Harris ... tell him I'm on my way. Then, Photography, Plan Drawing, Fingerprints, Forensic Science, Dog Section ... Billy Smart's Circus, if you think it'll help. Get 'em all out, and down there. The super ... get him from his kip. And every C.I.D. bloke who's on the end of a telephone wire. My compliments to 'em – all of 'em ... and, if they're not there, before I arrive, I'll have their goolies for croquet balls.'

A voice said, 'What an educated turn of phrase you have.'

'Eh?' Lennox replaced the receiver, and acknowledged the presence of his wife, who'd wandered in from the adjoining bedroom. He rumbled, 'They know what I mean, old pet.'

'Of course. *I* know what you mean – I wasn't brought up in a convent ... I merely object to being married to an oaf.'

Lennox trundled his obese body to where his clothes had been thrown, untidily, across the seat and back of an armchair.

His wife continued, 'I was beginning to hope the new rank might ...'

'A copper's been murdered,' wheezed Lennox, as he struggled to rid himself of the bed-socks.

'Oh!'

'I'll say "please" and "thank you", when we've nailed the bastard responsible.'

'I'm sorry,' said Mrs Lennox ... and meant it.

'Aye – so am I ... now, show how sorry you are, pet, by brewing a pot of tea, while I get dressed.'

Albert Quincey joined Emmerson, in the tiny dressing-room, as Emmerson rid himself of the uniform of his profession. The coloured man's movements were weary – almost lackadaisical – as he removed bow-tie, jacket and cummerbund; weary beyond the normal weariness of the o'clock; weary with something far beyond physical tiredness.

And, Quincey was sure he knew why.

'Bad night, Nic,' he observed, flatly.

'Yes, sir, Mr Quincey.'

'Not bad from the point of view of customers . . . I don't mean that.'

'No, sir.'

'For a Monday, not a bad night at all.'

'No, sir.'

'Good, in fact. Above average.'

'Yes, sir.'

'But the service – y'know . . . the service. Bad, Nic. Lousy.'

'If you say so, Mr Quincey,' said Emmerson, wearily.

'I'm meaning *you*, black man.' Quincey put an edge to his tone.

'Yes, sir, Mr Quincey. I guess you are.'

'I've seen better service from teenage bints in Woolworths.'

'Yes, sir,' sighed Emmerson.

'So, what gives, nigger?'

'I'm – I'm sorry, Mr Quincey.'

'And that's *it*?' sneered Quincey.

'I – I . . .'

'You being sorry. That squares everything, does it?'

'N-no, sir, Mr Quincey. It's just that . . .'

'You got things on your mind? That it?'

'Yes, sir,' breathed Emmerson, and moved his head in a defeated nod. 'I got a lot of things on my mind.'

Quincey grabbed the coloured man by the shoulder, spun him round and closed a fist on a handful of nylon shirt-front. He twisted his hand, and bent his arm, until Emmerson had to stand on tip-toe to stop himself from choking.

Tiny bubbles of spittle grew, then burst, at the corners of Quincey's mouth as he snarled, 'Listen to me, nigger. Listen good . . . 'cos I ain't gonna waste time repeating this.

These things – these things you have on your mind ... don't make any stupid decisions. Right? Think good. Think careful. 'Cos, you make the wrong decision, nigger, and you're gonna regret it, right up to the day they hide your black hide under a coffin lid. You get that? You make a wrong move – just *one* wrong move ... and you are gonna spend the rest of your lousy life wishing you were back, picking bloody cotton.'

Quincey straightened his bent arm, suddenly. He released the ball of nylon he was holding in his fist.

Emmerson catapulted backwards, and sprawled in a corner of the tiny dressing-room.

Quincey wiped the spittle clear with the back of a hand then, in a very matter-of-fact voice, said, 'You get the idea, Nic? You get the general message?'

Emmerson nodded, and whispered, 'Yes, sir, Mr Quincey. I get the message.'


That night, at fifteen minutes to two o'clock (an unearthly hour, by any yardstick) three people were abed, but not asleep. They each tried to sleep, but sleep refused them a visit.

The three people were Agatha Benson, Randal Alexander Osbert Joyce and James Crowe.


Miss Benson lay in the darkness of the only room in the world which she could, with any degree of honesty, call private and 'her own', and remembered.

Why?

The question intrigued her.

Why had she, a middle-aged spinster, acted the part of an awkward coquet? Why had she allowed – even encouraged – this man to invade her body? Why (despite her upbringing) had she had no shame? Why did she (now) have no regrets?

In the past (years ago) she had been ... *curious*. In stammered, badly worded innuendoes, she'd questioned her few married friends. They'd failed to understand (or had deliberately misunderstood) and her questions had remained unanswered. On an impulse (again, years ago) she'd bought a paperback edition of *The Perfumed Garden*. An unexpurgated edition. It had meant nothing. It had neither excited her nor nauseated her. It had certainly not repelled her ... although, at the time, she'd half-expected it to. Burton's prose style was far too pedantic for the subject-matter; like a cold-blooded academic explaining the various techniques of hysterectomy.

And, since then, the question had puzzled her. Half a lifetime – more than half a lifetime – and the mystery had remained a mystery. Was it really, as Burton suggested. Love-making – the act of copulation – was it *really* only a matter of contortions and rather childish parables? An exaggerated list of positions and similes?

Or was it (as the Brontë sisters suggested) something of the soul? An explosive emotion, not too far removed from a beautiful death?

Well, now she knew.

It was midway, between the two extremes – part-Burton, part-Brontë ... but beautiful, and exciting and never-to-be forgotten.

But the question remained unanswered.

Why – on this one day of her otherwise rather dreary life – had she suddenly decided to find out? Why? And why with a complete stranger? A stranger who was years younger than herself? A man she might never meet again? A man who (for all she knew) might, at this moment, be laughing at her, and laughing at the memory of an old maid who, for no logical

89

reason, had chosen *him* as a means of ridding herself of maidenhood?

Why?

Miss Benson was wrong, of course.

D.C. Joyce was *not* laughing. Indeed, D.C. Joyce's mind was hurting along similar tracks to her own and (like hers) at a tempo which pushed aside all thoughts of sleep.

I mean, she wasn't a beauty, for Christ's sake. She wasn't *beautiful*. Okay – she wasn't ugly ... she wasn't deformed, or anything like that. She was ...

We-ell, what *was* she?

She was the woman you pass a dozen times a day. The third, or fourth, woman you jostle in any supermarket. The woman you brake for, while she wanders across a pedestrian crossing.

She was so bloody ordinary ... as ordinary as *that*!

The hell she was ordinary.

In looks, maybe ... okay, in looks, she was ordinary. In dress, too – maybe ... okay, in dress, too, she was ordinary. But, nothing else was ordinary. Everything else was very *extra*-ordinary.

The way she talked, for instance. Simpering? – no, not simpering ... *shy*. Timid. A little like a fawn. As if she'd been brought up to be a little frightened of men. Wanting to please ... but forever frightened of displeasing.

Christ, what a difference.

What a difference between her, and the arse-swaying, smart-talking she-cats he usually laid. What a change from some of the foul-mouthed, my-crotch-is-as-important-as-yours crowd of libbers ... some of whom had damn near laid *him*.

She was ...

What *was* she?

90

She was a lady ... that's what she was. A lady who, at the same time, was one hell of a woman. She was *clean*. That was the only appropriate word. Clean. Unsullied. Bright, and shining, but in no way gaudy. In no way brash. In no way common. In no way, friend ... *in no way*!

The telephone, in the hall, interrupted his thoughts.

He swung out of bed, reached for his dressing-gown and threaded his arms through the sleeves. As he tied the sash he heard movement from his landlady's bedroom.

He called, 'Okay – I'll take it ... it's probably for me, anyway.'

It was.

It hauled him from his thoughts, and landed him smack in the eye of a murder enquiry.


Jim Crowe slept raw. The rough cotton sheets of the overnight transport stop were cool to his skin. Cool, and refreshing ... but, on this night, not conducive to slumber.

Jim Crowe had a whale of a lot of things on his mind.

He'd started by worrying about Pete ... then the worry had moved on to Nic ... and now, the worry was embracing Collins.

Ex-Chief Superintendent Collins ... ex-fuzz. Ex-Flight Lieutenant Collins ... ex-hero. Which? Which was the *real* Collins? Or, if they were both part of the complete Collins, what were the proportions? What was the mixture? How much of the old Collins was left in this new Collins?

That old Collins!

The Collins who, time and again, had led them in a modern Charge of the Heavy Brigade into, and out of, a twentieth-century Valley of Death.

The Ruhr.

Essen ... and Dusseldorf ... and Dortmund ...

\*    \*    \*

*All noise, all movement, all voices.*

*The earphones were filled with voices. Men's voices. Orders, more orders, instructions and more instructions. This was it! The reason for it all. Those terrifying minutes, over the target, when the Lanc shuddered, and bucked, and fought its way forward, like a man caught in the surge of a cup-final crowd. When it was no longer night; when even the small comfort of darkness was denied; when the flares and the markers gave light enough to see the score – hundreds – of black puffs from anti-aircraft shells, hurled up in a classic box-barrage.*

*No aiming. Those square-headed bastards below didn't aim. There was no need to aim. Just take a cubic area of sky and saturate it with anti-aircraft fire. Sling shells into that box, as fast as you could load and re-load. Fill the whole bloody box with exploding anti-aircraft shells ... and know that every Lanc had to punch its way through that box, before it could drop its bombs on target.*

*Some did. Some didn't ... and sometimes, on a bad night, a whole bloody squadron's kites didn't and, on such nights, every flier who'd ridden the target area knew the truth. That, on that night, jerry had come out on top. Well on top. A real, honest-to-God turkey-shoot, with anything up to three, or four, Lancs at a time exploding, or peeling off with their wings blazing, or fluttering down, like giant, wounded butterflies.*

*All noise, all movement, all voices.*

*The calm voice of the master-bomber, muffled in static and coming as if from another world.*

*'Main force. Master-bomber to main force. Come in, main force. Aim for the second red marker. Come on in, boys. It's all yours. Master-bomber to main force. Bomb-bomb. Bomb-bomb.'*

*Collins's voice, over the intercom. Tight and controlled*

*– a deliberate clipped drawl – part of being the skipper . . .
holding the lid on the mounting panic which could, so
easily, rip through the whole crew like a tidal bore.*

'Keep the chat to a minimum, boys. Five more minutes,
and we're out of it . . . leave the intercom to Ray and Johnny.'

*The voice of Johnny, the navigator.*

'Sixty seconds to target, skipper.'

'Come in, main force. Bomb-bomb. Bomb-bomb.'

*The voice of Ray, the bomb-aimer.*

'Left, skipper. Left – left . . . steady.'

'Fifty seconds.'

'Steady.'

'The second red marker, main force. The second red
marker. Ignore the first marker. Bomb for the second red
marker. Bomb-bomb. Bomb-bomb.'

'Forty seconds.'

*Alf's voice, from the mid-upper.*

'There's a Lanc coming in, from the left, skipper!'

'Got it, mid-upper. Thanks.'

'Left. Left, skipper! Left – left . . .'

'Thirty.'

'That's better, main force. Keep 'em coming. The second
red marker. Bomb-bomb. Bomb-bomb.'

'Skipper, that bloody Lanc's still . . .'

'Quiet, mid-upper. I have it.'

'Left, skipper. Left – left . . .'

'Come on in, main force. Don't drag your heels. The
second marker. The fire's around the second marker.'

'Skipper, I'm going to open fire on that bloody Lanc.
I'm . . .'

'Keep your fingers off those triggers, mid-upper!'

'Twenty seconds, skipper.'

'Left, skipper. Left!'

'Keep it coming, main force. Keep throwing for that second marker.'

'Left – left ... more left.'

'Skipper, if we get any closer ...'

'Get off the intercom, mid-upper.'

'Left, skipper. Left ... left.'

'Ten.'

'More left, skipper.'

'Nine.'

'Left – left ...'

'Eight.'

'Left ... steady.'

'Seven.'

'Steady, skipper.'

'Six.'

'Keep coming, main force.'

'Five.'

'Steady.'

'Four.'

'Left a little, skipper.'

'Three.'

'Steady ... steady.'

'Two.'

'Bomb-bomb, main force. Bomb-bomb.'

'One.'

'Bombs away, skipper ... let's get the hell out of here.'

All noise, all movement, all voices ... and now, the nose tilting down and the throttle levers rammed through the gates, and the Lanc quivering at every joint as it reached for an impossible speed with which to race through that bloody box-barrage.

And, a lifetime later, the Lanc banked and turned for home, and you breathed again – one long exhalation of sheer relief – and you relaxed the aching muscles of your

*jaw, and the aching muscles of your neck, and the aching
muscles of your shoulders ... the aching muscles of your
whole body. And, behind you – ten, twelve, fifteen thousand
feet below – a city blazed, and smoked and still exploded
... and you didn't give a damn because, in the face of all
odds, you were still alive.*

*And then Collins's voice. Still rigidly calm and controlled.
'Skipper here. Thanks.a lot, chaps. We're on our way
home, now. Gunners ... keep your eyes peeled for fighters.'*

*What a bloody way to fight a war. What a stupid, hare-
brained, suicidal, nerve-shredding way to fight a bloody war!*

*But (my Christ!) what a skipper.*

The old Collins. As indestructible as spring-steel. A man
with whom you cheerfully hocked your life, and a man
whose orders you obeyed ... even if the obeying of those
orders meant the forfeiture of your life.

Ex-Flight Lieutenant Collins ... ex-hero.

But, what about ex-Chief Superintendent Collins? ... ex-
fuzz?

What about *him*?


2.10 am ......


'Albert Hicks,' said Harris. 'Word's already out ... it was
circulated while you were on your way here.'

'Ah!' Lennox bobbed his bald head in acquiescence of
down-to-earth coppering. He didn't ask daft questions; if
Harris said 'Albert Hicks' – and, in the saying of that word,
implied that 'Albert Hicks' was the hound responsible for
the killing – that was good enough for Lennox. Therefore,

instead of asking daft questions, Lennox asked a very important question. He said, 'What about Mrs Davenport?'

'Her father was a sergeant, in the Met. Her brother's in the force – Salford ... we've already contacted 'em. A squad car's on the way.'

Once more, Lennox nodded his satisfaction.

Such a short exchange, and yet it told so much.

It emphasised the closing of the ranks, whenever a copper gets himself murdered; and not just the closing of the ranks within his own force ... the closing of the ranks within the whole of the British Police Service.

It underlined the peculiar, and unique, 'family' of which every policeman (and every policewoman), of whatever rank, is a part. A very select 'club', if you will ... and every wife, and every child, of every member of that 'club' is included in its membership.

Police Constable Davenport had been murdered. His killer could be named. Therefore (neck-and-neck priorities) the killer had to be grabbed, and the widow had to be told but, at the same time, saved as much pain in the telling as possible. That she had 'police blood' in her veins helped.

And now, the two big-wigs of Bordfield Regional Metropolitan Police District were, despite the hour, up and about, and organising things.

Harris ... Assistant Chief Constable (Crime). A big man; topping the six-foot mark, in his socks; a solid-looking man, with great slabs of meat anchored to a spine as stiff, and straight, as a tow-bar; heavy, but not fat, and with a mane of immaculately groomed white hair. His dress was a model for all senior detectives. Blue serge suit, complete with waistcoat. White shirt and sombre-coloured knotted tie. Unbelted mac. *Not* a bowler-hat – but only (and this was the impression) because such headgear was, these days, considered a mite eccentric ... therefore, Harris contented himself by being bareheaded.

Lennox ... Detective Chief Superintendent, and Head of Bordfield Region C.I.D. In looks, and dress, all a detective should *not* be; all a 1930's stand-up comic might have been expected to be. Fat, to the point of obesity. Completely bald, except for untamed whisps of grey hair, above his ears. And his clothes ... Ye Gods, his clothes! They changed each week and, each week, they grew fractionally more outrageous; fractionally more ridiculous. At this particular moment, for example, he wore trousers of a broad, grey-and-white check. He wore a bottle-green, Harris tweed, hacking-jacket, of 1940 vintage. He wore a Fair Isle pullover whose dazzling (but badly stained) colours were damn-near lethal, he wore a lumberjack shirt and a polka-dot bow-tie. On his head, he wore a cloth cap; a cloth cap which was (at a guess) a size-and-a-half too small for his skull and which (if appearances had anything to do with it) he'd positioned with extreme care, and the help of a spirit-level and plumb-line.

He looked an idiot.

He *wasn't* an idiot and, because he wasn't an idiot, Harris tolerated (even admired) him.

Having answered Lennox's questions, Harris noted his colleague's get-up, swallowed, then said, 'Superintendent James's office, I think.'

'Aye,' agreed Lennox. 'It's getting a bit crowded in here ... despite the floor space.'

And, indeed, it was.

For the first time since its opening, Bordfield Regional Metropolitan Police District Headquarters seemed to be an appropriate size for its number of occupants. Bobbies ... the impression was that they were arriving by the carton, and bumper-family-size packet. Uniformed, C.I.D. and men (and women) from the uniformed branch who'd arrived in civvies

97

because, while not being on duty, they'd been notified and had wanted to give whatever help they could. The so-called 'specialist services' ... Photography, Fingerprints, Plan Drawing, Criminal Intelligence, Forensic Science, Dog Section (complete with socking great, tail-wagging Alsatians). The Mounted Branch weren't there, nor was the Aqua-Section ... but only because there was no water, and there wasn't room for half-a-dozen horses! Constables, sergeants, inspectors, chief inspectors and Superintendent James, the uniformed can-carrier as far as the headquarters building itself was concerned. Motor patrol and foot patrol and those betwixt-and-between boys who tooled around their respective beats on glorified mopeds.

In the office (Superintendent James's office) things were less hectic. James, himself, was there, so was Harris and Lennox, so was the divisional detective inspector ... and the beat sergeant who'd found P.C. Davenport's body.

The beat sergeant was saying, '... and, with the cell keys being off their hook, I took it for granted he'd gone down to see Hicks. Hicks was the only customer, tonight. It had to be Hicks ... if Dave was down in the cells. Anyway – about a quarter of an hour, maybe less – I got worried. I wondered what was keeping him. So, I went down ... and that's when I found him.'

'What time was this?' asked Harris.

'Oh – about quarter to midnight ... it was ten to, when I got back upstairs. When I telephoned the inspector, to tell him – y'know ... to *tell* him.'

'What time did you go out on the street?'

'Just after eleven, sir. Ten past ... near as dammit.'

'There is,' said Harris, 'a Standing Instruction, in this force. No police station will be left manned by less than two officers, whilever a prisoner is in that police station's cells.'

'Yes, sir.' The sergeant looked miserable. 'But ...'

'Sir,' chipped in James, 'with respect – bearing in mind the present man-power problem – it's not a practical proposition.'

'Of course it ain't.' Lennox spoke, fractionally ahead of Harris. He turned to the unhappy sergeant, and said, 'It's one o' those things, old son. Mr Harris, here, is just reminding you ... see? Not criticising you. Those Force Standing Instructions ... we all break 'em. Just as long as we *know* we're breaking 'em ... that's the main thing.'

'I'm damned ...' began Harris.

'I mean,' expanded Lennox, 'if we went by *that* boss-eyed book, we'd need to have a piece of chalk, and draw bobbies on brick walls.'

'Yes, sir. Thank you, sir.'

The sergeant looked relieved.

Harris breathed heavily, then said, 'Time of death, then? Between eleven, and quarter-to-midnight?'

'Yes, sir.'

'Last bus services?'

'Very few after eleven, sir. None, after eleven-thirty.'

'Trains?'

'That, I wouldn't be sure about, sir. All night ... if you're not going anywhere in particular.'

'You know this Hicks character?' said Lennox.

'Yes, sir.'

'Right.' Lennox jerked his head. 'Pick up three men. Get to the City Station ... fast. Enquiries about whether he's already left ... if so, where for. Search the station ... especially the bogs. Then, stay there, till you're relieved, in case it's where he's making for.'

The sergeant said, 'Yes, sir,' and left the office.

'He's a Bordfield man, sir,' said the D.D.I. 'One of the local tearaways ... I've got men watching his house, already.'

Harris and James spoke together.

Harris said, 'Photographs?'

James said, 'He won't go home . . . after killing a police officer.'

'Ah, but if he *does* go home,' murmured Lennox.

'I beg your pardon?' James looked puzzled.

'We'll look like so many soft-boiled eggs, if somebody isn't waiting for him.'

'Ah – er – yes . . . of course. It wasn't that I . . .'

'Photographs,' repeated Harris, doggedly. 'Do we have any?'

'Last time he was inside,' the D.D.I. said. 'That's about two years back. He was photographed and fingerprinted, then.'

'He hasn't grown whiskers . . . anything like that?'

'No, sir.'

'So, he won't have changed all that much. Get onto Records – we want the negative at Photography, as soon as possible, then – what do you think, Lenny . . . a hundred?'

'Two hundred,' said Lennox. 'Let's go wild – give the cat another goldfish . . . and postcard size.'

'Two hundred, postcard size,' said Harris. 'And ready for distribution before six.'

'Will do,' said the D.D.I., and he, too, hurried from the office.

'And that,' said Lennox, 'leaves the late-night buses, the taxi firms and nicked cars. If we can eliminate *them*, he's still in the city . . . and all we have to do is find him.'

'We'll find him.' Harris's tone was hard, flat and as uncompromising as a hangman's trap. 'Whichever rat-hole he's bolted down . . . we'll find him.'


Forty-seven Christopher Crescent . . . *that* was the rat-hole.

'You wanna see your kid again, get me outa here.'

Emmerson believed him.

It was one of the nights of Emmerson's life. The glowering frightened (but terrifyingly dangerous) Hicks; a roughneck, with nothing to lose, and a roughneck who held Emmerson's son – Emmerson's whole future – in the palm of his hand. Emmerson didn't doubt this ... he didn't *dare* doubt it.

Therefore, Emmerson gave Hicks the sanctity of his home. They sat, silent, for hours on end. Each afraid, and each with his own fear. The gas fire hissed the small hours through, until dawn and, for most of the time, its glow was the only illumination Hicks allowed in the curtained room. The warmth from the fire was only partial; the first frost of winter sent chilling draughts through chinks in badly-fitted doors. Occasionally, and in the distance, they heard the rise and fall of police sirens, and Hicks leaned forward in his chair, like an animal ready to spring, while Emmerson sent a silent prayer to his own, very personal, God ... 'It ain't easy, God. Just sitting here, with this man. This man, who's gonna kill Pete if I don't do what he says. It ain't easy. It ain't even right ... and don't think I don't know that. I should do something. For the sake of Pete, I should do something. Maybe run out in the street, and yell. Attract the neighbours. Get the police here, somehow. That's what I should do, God ... and don't think I don't know it. But, it's Pete ... see? Pete! Suppose I do it all wrong. Suppose I make a mistake. I ain't that clever – you know that – and I could easy make a mistake. Then what? What about Pete, then? I need to think about Pete. I promised Daisy. You know that ... you was there, at the time. I promised Daisy and, if I do the wrong thing, she ain't never gonna forgive me. I ain't never gonna forgive myself. So – y'know ... keep the police away from here. Eh? Just till ... things happen. Something. I ain't asking a lot, God. I ain't asking for no miracle. Just that nothing happens. That's all. It ain't easy, just sitting here. But, that's okay. I ain't complaining. Just so nothing happens ... that's all.'

Two men.

Each afraid.

Each reaching towards a new day, in the lonely company of his own fear.

2.30 am until 6.30 pm ......

It is shown on television, it is written about in books, it is reflected, in glorious Technicolor, on the cinema screen. The man-hunt; the cops, in full cry; the jacks, doing their 'thing'. Sometimes these fairy tales are written by (or, perhaps, vetted by) men who know their onions and, occasionally, they approximate the truth ... but, *always*, with baubles attached.

The real truth is, the baubles just aren't there!

Bobbies are the most unglamorous creatures on earth, performing the most unglamorous profession ever thought up by man. They cold-bloodedly hound the rogues of their own species. They have mathematical minds; they take two, add a second two, and come up with an immaculate four ... and, if they come up with less than four, they know that one of the original brace of twos was short-weight, and that it's a waste of time dumping that little lot in the Scales of Justice, because the balance will be all wrong. They have the obstinacy, and staying-power, of a camel; they can travel up to one hundred hours (plus), without sleep and on a spasmodic diet of cheap tea and fags ... which is why ulcers, coronary back-flips and general internal screw-ups are, to all intents and purposes, their major 'industrial diseases'. They have the imagination of a battery-fed hen; they can be licked, brow-beaten, smashed and decimated, without even feeling the draught ... which, be it whispered, in no way helps marital harmony and, if 'the police mind' is ever judicially recognised as an instrument of mental cruelty, the queue of fed-up women waiting outside any divorce court is likely to be three deep.

Bobbying – not so much a way of life ... more a matter of masochistic vocation!

And the definitive period of any copper's life-style is when he seeks the killer of his kind.

The Bordfield coppers went mad in that four-hour period, between 2.30 am and 6.30 am. They ringed Hicks's home so tightly, a stray cat couldn't have broken the cordon unnoticed. They went through his belongings, like an army of soldier-ants and, when the indignant Mrs Hicks made noises of outraged objection, they pushed her aside and went through *her* knick-knacks, too. They roused Hicks's mates, and his fancy women, from their slumbers. They asked questions and, when those questions were answered, they disbelieved the answers, on principle. They opened scores of cupboards – scores of drawers – and, from hundreds of notebooks and pieces of paper, they copied names and addresses. Then, they visited people and places, culled from those names and addresses, in their search for the whereabouts of Hicks.

The Bordfield coppers went mad; mad with cold, furious insanity which rips through every force whenever one of its members is done to death.

And (almost coincidentally) Detective Constable Joyce stumbled across the thread which linked a known crime to an unknown crime.

Joyce's enquiries took him to the taxi firms, and one of the taxi firms was City Taxis.

In the radio room, the man with the eye-patch, and the scars across his face, still sat at the table, within reach of the microphone. A transistor was tuned to a foreign station, and German opera fought a losing battle with modern pop and a French disc-jockey.

The eye-patched man looked up, with mild disinterest, as Joyce entered the room.

He said, 'You find out why, then?'

'I beg your pardon?'

'Len ... you find out why he took the Morris out there, and set fire to it?'

'Oh – er – no.' Joyce hitched a cheek of his backside onto a corner of the table, glanced at the transistor, and said, 'Would it be asking too much?'

'Wassat?'

'This is serious. A certain amount of concentration is essential.'

'About Len, and the ...'

'No ... about murder. Specifically, about the murder of a police officer.'

The man with the eye-patch took the news stone-faced, reached across, turned off the transistor, then said, 'Wagner couldn't write a good tune, if his next meal depended on it, anyway. Why should Len murder a copper?'

'Eh?' Joyce stared.

'Why should he murder anybody?'

'Who?'

'Len. Len Garfield. He's slightly cross-threaded ... okay. But I wouldn't say he's ...'

'Not Garfield.' Joyce caught up with the chit-chat. 'No – not Garfield ... you misinterpreted my words, I'm afraid. Hicks. A man called Albert Hicks. We'd like to know ...'

'Bert Hicks?'

'Yes ... Bert Hicks.' Joyce felt the hairs at the nape of his neck tingle.

'He's *definitely* cross-threaded.'

'You know the man?'

'We've used him.'

'Er ... used him? As a driver?'

'Not me.' The man with the eye-patch shook his head in disgust. 'Lipton ... the bloke you saw earlier. He's used Hicks, once or twice.'

'Used?' insisted Joyce.

'Taxi-war,' explained the man with the eye-patch.

'Oh!'

'When the mini-cab clowns tried to trespass. We needed a thumper. Hicks came in handy.'

'You haven't seen him this evening? Tonight at any time? Hicks, I mean?' Having asked the triple-question, Joyce held his breath.

'Not for weeks,' said the man with the eye-patch.

'Oh!'

'I think Garfield sees him, sometimes.'

'What brings you to that conclusion?'

'He mentions him ... sometimes.'

'In what way?'

'Just – y'know ...' The man with the eye-patch shrugged. 'The name. Bert Hicks. He drops it, now and again. As if they bump into each other, sometimes.'

Joyce nodded, then said, 'If he comes in, tonight – at any time – if he contacts you in any way – nine-nine-nine. He's killed a copper. We want him ... badly.'

'Hicks?'

'Hicks.'

'I'm not surprised. He's *definitely* cross-threaded.'

It was a lead – even a promising lead – and Joyce followed it. His next stop was Billings Lane, where he awakened

Garfield's landlady, and was told that Garfield hadn't been seen by her since breakfast the previous day ... and no, she didn't know where he was ... and no, she didn't know anybody called Albert Hicks.

End of lead.

Joyce sighed, then continued his round of taxi firms. The link between Hicks, Garfield and City Taxis was worth a short report (when he had time enough to sit down at a type-writer) but no more.


6.30 am ......


The *exact* time was 6.32 am. And, police training being what it is, the exact time was noted. 6.32 am ... when the pick-up swerved to miss a wandering dog, skidded on the frost-coated tarmac and purled into a concrete lamp-stand-ard at a steady fifty miles per hour. *Exactly* 6.32 am ... because, the city being stiff with squad cars, the two motor patrol officers in the squad car actually *witnessed* the acci-dent, and were on the scene within seconds.

It doesn't often happen like that, but it did this time.

And it had seemed such a good idea.

Emmerson had spent all night thinking up, then dis-carding, schemes for getting Hicks clear of the city boun-daries. It had to be done ... Pete's life depended on it.

Then he'd remembered his neighbour, the greengrocer.

He'd borrowed the pick-up; he'd told lies about fictitious urgencies, fictitious members of his family and fictitious illnesses. Maybe Ted hadn't believed the lies – that wasn't important – but he'd loaned him the pick-up.

Hicks had secreted himself under a tarpaulin, in the

body of the vehicle, and Emmerson had pushed the accelerator hard down in the near-empty streets.

Then had come the dog, the frosted tarmac and the concrete lamp-standard.

One of the motor patrol officers sent the message back to Bordfield H.Q. Radio Control Room.

'Baker Foxtrot Twenty-six to Control. You can call off the pack. We've found Hicks.'

'Control to Baker Foxtrot Twenty-six. Be a little more specific, please.'

'He was making a run for it, in the back of a pick-up truck. The truck skidded into a lamp-post ... and, you'll be pleased to know, rigor mortis is already setting in.'

'Dead?'

'As a stuck pig. Looks like his neck hit the steel side of the truck. Heads aren't supposed to be stuck on at *that* angle ... if you see what I mean.'

'Hang about, mate. We'll need medical verification.'

'Of course. But, I've seen enough stiffs.'

'Champion. Who was driving?'

'A coloured gent. He's still alive ... just. His skull smashed the windscreen.'

'Not to worry. They have thick skulls.'

'They tell me.'

'Anyway, hang on there, mate. I'll blow for the blood-wagon, and have some help with you, as soon as possible.'

'Right. Nice, though ... isn't it? The bastard who did for poor old Davenport has got his, already.'

'It's known as justice, mate. Justice.'

But, it *wasn't* justice ... not by a light-year.

It was trouble.

Big trouble.

107

'We've got trouble, skipper. We've got big trouble.'

Crowe looked as worried as any man can look, as he sat on the stool, in Collins's kitchen, and told his tale of woe.

'The greengrocer's quite sure?' queried Collins.

'Yeah. It's his truck.'

'Quite.' Collins munched buttered toast and sipped coffee. He said, 'Come on, James. Have *some* breakfast. Fasting won't help.'

'Honest to God, skip. I couldn't.'

'You can.' Collins pushed the toast-rack a fraction of an inch across the Formica top of the breakfast-bar. He said, 'Now, why on earth should your brother-in-law be driving a man like Hicks?'

'Search me, skip.'

'I know this man, Hicks. He's a bad hat.'

'Yeah. If he's killed a copper ...'

'It wasn't accidental. Whatever the surrounding circumstances, it wasn't accidental.'

'So, why the hell was Nic ...'

'I was hoping you might be able to tell me.'

'No.' Crowe shook a miserable head. 'It don't make sense, skipper. With a guy like Nic ...'

'Unless, of course, it's linked up with the kidnapping.'

'Yeah,' sighed Crowe.

'Eat some breakfast, James.'

'Skipper, how the hell can I ...'

'Because I tell you to. And because, if we're back together as a team, one of us has to *obey* orders.'

Crowe hesitated. For a moment, it seemed as if he might slip his angry frustration.

'James!' murmured Collins, softly. Warningly.

Crowe's face relaxed into a wry, twisted grin, and he reached for toast and moved the cup of freshly poured coffee a little nearer.

There was a silence then, in a deceptively throw-away tone, Collins said, 'The police are in. We'd be fools not to use them.'

'Hey, skipper ...'

'Not officially, of course.'

'Eh?'

'They're human, James. I speak from experience.'

'Yeah, but ...'

'Pick the right man. Insist that he be – er – "off duty" ... and he'll respect your confidences.'

'Yeah ... the right man,' agreed Crowe, without enthusiasm.

'I know him,' drawled Collins.

'The right man?'

'Oh, my word.' Collins chuckled. 'He'll love it. He'll wallow in it ... and, come to think of it, "wallow" is a very appropriate word.'

'If you're sure, skipper. If you're absolutely *sure*.'

Collins let the remark slide past him; he treated it as if it wasn't worthy of an answer.

He popped the last of the toast into his mouth, chewed, swallowed, then sipped coffee, before he said, 'Now – this greengrocer ... he didn't ask for your name?'

'No ... and he didn't get it.'

'We can assume your brother-in-law is in hospital.'

'With a cop at his bedside.'

'And, as his next-of-kin ... you are his next-of-kin, I hope?'

'Apart from Pete.'

'Good. As his next-of-kin, you obviously require to see him. To ask after his health.'

'They ain't gonna let anybody see the poor guy. After what they figure he's done? They ain't gonna ...'

'Strings,' murmured Collins.

'Eh?'

'Strings, James. Strings, as thick as guy-ropes. They're there to be pulled, when necessary. They'll *be* pulled ... I give you my word. Now, finish your toast, drink your coffee and stop worrying. We have a trip to make ... to a cattery.'

'A what?'

'A cattery. A place where they breed Russian Blues. Beautiful cats. All cats are beautiful ... but Russian Blues are *particularly* beautiful.'


The youth lay as still as death. Any movement might have disturbed the springs of the ancient bed; might have been heard in the silence of the echoing farmhouse. And the youth was listening – straining his ears to catch every word of one part of a telephone conversation – and, from what he heard, build answers to a score of questions.

Garfield's voice came up, through the well of the stairs, from the hall, and names were named and remarks were made and, from the names and the remarks, the outline of an overall picture came gradually to be glimpsed.

Garfield's voice was saying, '... without a radio. And newspapers aren't delivered here, until nearly noon. So, how can I have heard the ...... Oh, my God! ...... You're sure? Well, thank God for small mercies, but ...... Look, Al, I can't do that ...... Not on my own. I need somebody else. I can't ...... How the hell *can* I? ...... Sure. It's all right for you. You're in the clear. You're not ...... Not on my own, Al. Not on my own! No way ...... Christ, it's cocked itself up. Can't you see that? ...... All right, but what happens if the old man croaks? Where does that leave me? ...... I talk, Al. You'd better believe that. If I'm caught, I don't suck the whole hammer. Hicks was in it. You're in it. It was a three-way split ...... Okay, now it's a two-way, but you'd better get something moving. Fast. 'Cos, if I'm caught, I talk, man. Don't kid yourself. I talk ...... Okay. But, do that. And fast.'

The youth heard the click of the receiver being replaced on its prongs.

Then, footsteps on stone flags.

The footsteps halted.

A man's voice said, 'Well?'

'Hicks is dead.'

A woman's voice asked, 'How?'

'Some sort of road accident. He killed a lawman ... maybe they were chasing them. I dunno.'

'Them?' asked the woman's voice.

'Emmerson was driving ... that's what I'm told.'

The youth stiffened, and suddenly felt the cold touch of true fear.

'Emmerson?' The woman's voice held disbelief and shock.

'I dunno. I dunno what the hell's happened.'

The woman's voice said, 'Get him out of here. We want him out of here.'

'Where? How the hell can I ... ?'

'We want him out of here. Today. This morning.'

'Al's going to ...'

'I don't want to know. Neither of us wants to know ... anything else.'

'Don't be crazy, woman.'

The voices became louder, as anger took over.

The woman's voice snapped, 'At twelve, noon, I telephone

**III**

the police. If you're still here, they'll know where to find you.'

'And *you*?'

'We'll be all right.'

'Oh, yes. Sure.' Garfield's voice held furious scorn. 'You only provided bed and board ... that's all. You're so bloody innocent, the halo must hurt.'

'Noon,' snapped the woman's voice.

The man's voice added, 'We were forced to do it. That's what we'll say ... that you threatened us. They'll believe us ... just as long as they get their hands on you.

The talking stopped, and the youth heard footsteps climb the stairs.

As Garfield entered the bedroom, the youth closed his eyes and pretended to be asleep.

Garfield said, 'Pete,' and his voice was soft, and almost sad.

The youth kept his eyes closed.

'Pete.' Garfield touched the youth's shoulder, and shook it, gently. 'Pete ... time to get up.'

'Eh?' The youth opened his eyes and pretended to awaken. He blinked, and said, 'What time is it?'

'Just after eight. Time to get up, Pete.'

'Where ...' The youth play-acted; he glanced round the room with mock-mystification.

'It's okay, Pete.' Garfield raised a tired smile, as far as his mouth corners. 'You remember things now ... eh?'

'You've – you've been in touch with daddy?' asked the youth, innocently.

'Not – er ... no, not yet.'

'When?'

'Soon. Maybe today.'

'He'll be worried,' said the youth.

'Yeah ... I – er – I guess he will. I would be.'

The youth glanced down at the leg-iron, then said, 'Let me go. I won't tell them.'

'Would you?' asked Garfield, ruefully.

'What?'

'In my position. Would *you* take that risk?'

'I don't tell lies, Mr Garfield.'

'No ... I'm not calling you a liar, Pete.'

'Well, then?'

'Be practical, son.' Garfield's tone was heavy with near-defeat. 'I'm over the ears in this thing. I can't take the risk.'

'There's no risk. I'd ...'

'And I need the bread,' added Garfield in a harsher voice. 'I need the bread, bad. More than you. More than your old man. I need it!'

'I'll tell him,' offered the youth. 'I'll explain. I'll make him understand.'

Garfield shook his head.

'Please,' pleaded the youth.

'No way, Pete. So, knock it off ... eh? If I lose you, I'm *really* nailed to the floor.'

'I think you're being silly, Mr Garfield,' said the youth, sombrely. 'I think you're being very silly ... and very wicked.'

Garfield's voice was flat and expressionless, as he said, 'Yeah. I'm a bastard, kid. The world's full of bastards, like me ... you'd better learn it. That way, you survive.'


9.30 am ......


'The Egyptians,' said Mrs Lennox. 'The Felis caffra. Not, as some ignorant people think, the Felis catus. The European

113

wild cat – the Felis catus – isn't at *all* like the domesticated cat. It's far larger. Far more powerful. Definitely the Felis caffra, from ancient Egypt.'

'I see,' said Collins, politely.

Crowe was a little less polite.

He said, 'They're all cats, to me, ma'am.'

'You're like my husband,' snapped Mrs Lennox, irritably. 'Moggies ... that's what he calls them. Moggies! He's an uneducated lout. I only hope *you* don't call them moggies.'

'No, ma'am ... I wouldn't dare.'

Collins suppressed a smile, and wondered when Lennox would arrive home. He had (according to his wife) telephoned, almost half an hour ago, to say he was on his way; to instruct her to prepare a meal for a hungry, yet contented, man.

Since their arrival, and while they waited for the return of the master of the house, they'd talked cats and looked at cats. Mainly Russian Blues (of which Mrs Lennox was one of the top northern breeders), but also cross-bred tabbies ... mere 'cats', and not aristocrats of their species who, in this solid, severely-dressed woman, had recognised a never-ending meal ticket.

They strolled from the runs and cages, towards the rear of the house itself; a rambling, stone building, with steep-pitched roofs and mullioned windows; an early nineteenth-century structure, standing in its own two acres, and surrounded by open fields and coppices. Severe, and yet not forbidding, it had character – the sort of character associated with steel-stiff presbyters, with marsh-mallow hearts – and obviously cost a bomb to heat ... but (as Collins mentally mused) when you add the income derived from breeding prize-winning kittens, to the salary of a detective chief superintendent, massive heating bills can be met without undue hardship.

All the way back to the house, Mrs Lennox chatted 'cat talk'.

Collins and Crowe made polite noises, at appropriate moments, but weren't too interested.

As Mrs Lennox closed the rear door, Lennox entered at the front.

Lennox bawled, 'Food, my pet. Food, for the starving workers. And not gruel. None of your wishy-washy ...' He rounded a corner in the corridor, leading from the hall, saw the visitors for the first time, grinned expansively, and said, 'Henry, old cock. That's nice ... that's a nice surprise. I saw the car, parked out front, and thought it was some berk here to buy a mog.' He glanced at Crowe, then added, '*Is* it? Sorry, old son. Is that why you're here? If so, they're wonderful cats. The best money can buy ... even if they are a bit on the high side.'

'Not cats, Lenny,' smiled Collins.

'Good ... I ain't dropped a clanger, after all.'

'What do you want for breakfast?' asked Mrs Lennox, tightly.

'Not gruel. What the hell your pal says, gruel's no food for a growing man.'

'What? Bacon sandwiches?'

'Are you up to it?'

'Are you suggesting ...'

'All right, luv. Bacon sandwiches. Nice and crisp, though ... eh?'

'I'll see to them ... oaf.'

Mrs Lennox flounced through a door, leading to the kitchen.

Lennox beamed at Collins and Crowe, and said, 'She's a good wife. A bit barmy on cats ... but a good wife.'

'Of course,' murmured Collins.

Crowe remained silent.

The fact was that the obese, ridiculously dressed Lennox was something he wouldn't have believed without the evidence of his own eyes. A cop? Some cop! A pantomime comedian – sure ... by all means. But not a *cop*.

'It's about Hicks,' said Collins, gently.

'Oh, aye?' Lennox flicked an internal switch, and the beam left his face. The rosebud mouth tightened into a thin line and a film of ice seemed to grow over the slightly bulbous eyes. He growled, 'He killed a copper ... y'know that?'

Collins nodded.

'He's dead. Good riddance. Hicks, I mean ... not the copper.'

'A van, I believe,' said Collins.

'A pick-up.'

'And the man who was driving him?'

Lennox looked hard at Crowe, then said, 'A coloured. Henry, old mate, bells are ringing.'

'Same skin pigmentation,' said Collins, mildly. 'Let me introduce you. James – James Crowe ... Emmerson's brother-in-law. James ... Detective Chief Superintendent Lennox.'

They shook hands. Crowe was surprised at the firmness of the grip of the podgy fingers.

Lennox rumbled, 'Well ... what next?'

'Not unless we're off the record, Lenny,' said Collins.

Lennox rubbed a hand across his billiard-ball head, and muttered, 'I dunno about that, Henry. If you know summat ...'

'You have the murderer.'

'Aye.'

'And the driver.'

'Aye.'

'As far as the killing of the constable's concerned, what more do you want?'

116

'Nothing,' agreed Lennox.

'And Emmerson?'

'He's nailed ... you know that, Henry. Trying to drive a killer to some sort of safety. He hasn't a leg to stand on.'

'Especially if it isn't a white leg,' said Crowe, grittily.

'Come again, son.' Lennox switched his attention to Crowe, and the voice belied the comical appearance of its owner.

'Black,' said Crowe, harshly. 'He's as guilty as hell, because he's black.'

'You're a pal of *my* pal,' growled Lennox. 'Otherwise you'd get my boot up your backside, for that remark.'

'What else? You've tried him ...'

'Don't talk like a flaming idiot.'

' "Guilty as hell" – the words you just used ... you've already tried him, in your own mind. Nothing else matters.'

'He'll be charged.'

'Fixed.'

'If he's guilty, he'll be punished.'

'He already *is* guilty. You've just said.'

'*If* he's guilty.'

'Hey, fuzz, you've already decided.'

'Don't be a damn fool ...'

'You ain't never gonna take "No" for an answer.'

'... it was a figure of speech.'

'Go screw yourself, copper.'

'Look – sonny – watch that mouth of yours.'

'Go screw yourself.' Crowe turned to Collins, and snapped, 'I'll be in the car. Go ahead ... carve Nic up, with fatso.'

'James!'

'I'll be in the car, skipper. If I stay, I'm likely to puke.'

Crowe strode angrily to the hall, and slammed the front door as he left the house.

Lennox blew out his cheeks, then said, 'And what the thundering hell brought *that* rush of blood to the head?'

'Off the record?' said Collins, smoothly.

'With a lunatic like that? You must be joking.'

'You'll regret it, Lenny.'

'All my life,' said Lennox, wearily. 'The things I regret ... I wish I had as many pound notes.'

'I'm serious, Lenny.'

'Look – Henry ... that pal of yours. What's his name? ... Crowe. He used words, then put them in *my* mouth. Right? "Guilty as hell" ... they were *his* words, not mine. I don't work that way. I don't ...'

'He doesn't know that.'

Lennox snorted, then said, 'In that case, he'll bloody well find out, won't he? And when he does ...'

'Tell me,' said Collins, smoothly, 'why *did* Hicks murder the constable?

'Davenport? P.C. Davenport?'

'Why did Hicks murder him?' repeated Collins.

'To make his escape ... presumably,' grunted Lennox.

'What was he in for?' asked Collins, innocently.

'Hicks?'

'If you don't mind telling me. What was the charge?'

'G.B.H. Some sorta pub brawl. He grabbed a handful of darts, and shoved 'em into another bloke's face.'

'Another tearaway?'

'As always.' Lennox nodded, and his jowls wobbled. 'I don't have to tell you, Henry. They're a blasted nuisance. A good sniff o' the barman's apron, and they're away ... fighting drunk.'

'I find that odd,' mused Collins.

'What?'

Mrs Lennox joined them. She was carrying a giant tray, upon which were three mugs of steaming tea, a large teapot, sugar, milk and a plate of sandwiches.

She looked puzzled, and said, 'I expected your friend, Mr Crowe being ...'

'Thank you Mrs Lennox.' Collins smiled. 'That's very thoughtful of you ... but he's stepped outside, for a moment.'

'Oh, I see.'

'In the study, pet,' rumbled Lennox.

Collins stepped forward and opened a door leading from the corridor.

'Some people,' said Mrs Lennox, acidly, 'even have manners.'

'Eh?' Lennox blinked, owlishly.

'You wouldn't know what I mean.'

'No ... to tell you the truth, I don't.'

'Eat ... pig,' snapped Mrs Lennox, as she dumped the tray on a massive refectory table, which stood in the centre of the large room, and did combined duty as desk and dining-table.

She left the room, and closed the door with studied deliberation.

Lennox stared at the closed door, then said, 'I dunno ... honest I don't. Queer? I sometimes think she's up the pole. I reckon it must be all those bloody cats.'

The rain started. Hesitantly. Spot at a time; huge, five-pence-piece spots which hit the sloping windscreen, held their own with gravity for a moment, then reluctantly crawled down the glass and spread themselves along the rubber surround.

They reminded him ...

The raindrops brought back memories. Memories of Collins ... the old Collins. Memories of happier, but more terrifying, days ...

\*     \*     \*

119

*Five Group, Bomber Command. 'Cochrane's Young Ladies'.*
*But, also, 'The Pathfinders for The Pathfinders'. 'The Glory*
*Group' ... with all the household names Bomber Command.*
*Gibson, Martin and Maudslay. Shannon, Young and Knight.*
*Fauquier, Tait and Cheshire. Maltby, Trevor-Roper and*
*Foxlee.*

*Those men. Those machines. Those Lancasters. To be*
*even a tiny part of their mystique was to have a pride, beyond*
*all normal pride. To have flown in the company of giants. To*
*be one of the recognised elite of Harris's massive bomber*
*force.*

*A gunner. An 'arse-end Charlie'. One of the best of the*
*best.*

*No Perspex in the rear turrets of Five Group. In Five*
*Group, the gunners sat there, surrounded by skeleton frame-*
*work, from which the Perspex had been removed. Fronted*
*by four .303 Brownings and a reflector sight. Catching the*
*slipstream's side-blast. Periodically kneading the rubber of*
*their oxygen tubes to clear the internal ice. Guns electrically*
*heated ... because that temperature froze gun-oil! Inner*
*flying-suits electrically heated ... and if the heating goofed,*
*the gunner grew cold, then tired and, finally, slept a sleep*
*from which he wouldn't awaken.*

*It had happened – too many times ... so the mid-uppers*
*kept their eyes on the rear turrets and, if the search stopped*
*(port-to-starboard, starboard-to-port, port-to-starboard, star-*
*board-to-port) they called the arse-ender on the intercom,*
*just to make sure.*

*No Perspex. Because, when they flew through cloud, lazy*
*droplets of moisture gathered on the curved surface of*
*Perspex and quivered in the rush of air and, more than once,*
*tired eyes had mistaken them for an attacking fighter ...*
*and battles had been fought against an imaginary foe.*

*So-o ... no Perspex.*

*Just a platform – an exposed dickey-seat – perched at the very end of a bloody great Lancaster bomber.*

The talk came in spurts; sentence at a time, with gaps of silence between. There was as much silence as there was talk ... possibly more. But every word meant something, and was carefully examined by the receiver before he, in turn, sent meaningful words back to the other.

They sipped tea, as they conversed – hot tea, and tea strong enough to fight the mellowing effect of milk and sugar and win – and Lennox chewed his way through bacon sandwiches.

'Hicks,' murmured Collins.

'He worked hard to keep us in business. That's about all anybody can say about him.'

'Quite.'

'You knew him?'

'Of him. He visited Lessford a few times.'

'High jinks?'

'We discouraged him. Not me – personally ... Sullivan, I think.'

'So, you'll know what sort of a turd he was.'

'Oh, yes.'

'Still ... I'd have given him credit for more gumption.'

'Than what?' asked Collins, smoothly.

'Killing a copper.'

'Why did he?' enticed Collins, with a half-smile.

'I dunno ... to get away, I suppose.'

'Drunk?'

'I doubt it. An hour in a police cell sobers 'em up.'

'Then, why? Why kill a police officer?'

'To – er – to get away. I reckon.'

'You don't sound *quite* convinced, Lenny.'

'He was on a G.B.H. sheet ... plus.'

'A public house brawl.'

'Aye . . . a pub set-to.'

Collins said, 'It wouldn't have gone to Crown Court. Not even with his record.'

'No . . . I reckon not. The local bench. That's about all.'

'Six months . . . maximum.'

'Aye.'

'And, to dodge that, he hands himself a life sentence?'

'Looks like it. He took the risk.'

'He'd spent years in prison.'

'Aye.'

'Six months would have meant nothing.'

Through half-chewed sandwich, Lennox mumbled, 'They don't think like we think, Henry old son. They're on a different wavelength.'

'But they *do* think.'

'I reckon . . . in their own potty fashion.'

'I could,' said Collins, airily, 'suggest a better motive.'

'For killing Davenport?'

'A much more urgent motive.'

Lennox swilled tea, noisily, then said, 'We ain't interested in motive, Henry. He's on a slab . . . where he belongs. We ain't even gonna shove him in a dock. That's nice. It saves money. We know he's the bastard – we can mark the file "Detected" with an easy conscience . . . that's it, mate. If they all came as easily as that, I wouldn't grumble.'

'Unless your name happened to be Davenport,' murmured Collins.

'Easy, mate.' Grit entered Lennox's tone. 'You know what I mean.'

Collins said, 'I know you haven't a motive worth mentioning.'

'The hell with his motive.'

'Fear?' suggested Collins, gently.

'I'm not frightened of any ...'

'Not you, Lenny. Hicks.'

'Cocky, you're playing your old game,' said Lennox, suspiciously. 'You're talking in riddles.'

'Fear,' repeated Collins. 'Fear of being in custody. Fear that he might be implicated in something far worse than G.B.H.'

'What? ... for example.'

'G.B.H. isn't *so* uncommon,' teased Collins. 'Six months – to a man like Hicks – isn't *so* unacceptable.'

'What?' rumbled Lennox.

'Off the record, of course,' smiled Collins.

Lennox rubbed the nape of his neck, and said, 'I have an impression, old cock.'

'Really?'

'That you're flogging me a stumer.'

'You've a suspicious mind, Lenny.'

'Aye ... that's what I'm paid for.'

'Lenny! *Would* I?'

'Yes, mate ... you would. And with a smile on your face while you're doing it.'

'Old friend, you know me better than that.'

' "Old friend" ... that's exactly how well I *do* know you.'

'I could take that as an insult.'

'You could ... but you ain't going to.'

'No?'

'Not if you want whatever it is you're after.'

'You're hurting my feelings, Lenny.'

'And *that'll* be the day!'

Collins chuckled, quietly ... as if at a secret joke.

Lennox frowned. The frown deepened into a scowl, then the scowl took on the air of a man sorely tempted.

Collins waited.

Lennox growled, 'Henry – joking apart ... you wouldn't be having me on, would you?'

'No.' Collins shook his head with great solemnity.

'Leading me up the garden path, till we reach the duck pond?'

'I'm talking about crime, Lenny.'

'I gathered that.'

'Big crime. Crime, big enough to scare a man like Hicks into murdering a policeman, rather than risk being found out.'

'But – er ... off the record. Right?'

'For the moment.'

'Why?'

'When I tell you, you'll know why.'

'And, if I listen, and then don't agree ... what then?'

Collins touched his lips with a finger, then said, 'Lenny, *unless* you agree, you won't have the chance to listen. You won't be told.'

'That's a hell of a dangerous thing to say, old cock.'

'No ... I don't think so.'

'Obstructing coppers?'

'Really?' Collins raised surprised eyebrows.

'Maybe even "Accessory After".'

'Of what?'

'Crime, for Christ's sake.'

'What crime?' asked Collins, softly.

'Eh?'

'Which crime are you investigating, Lenny?'

'Oh!'

'Or – if you like – which "investigation" am I obstructing?'

'I knew it!' Lennox blew out his cheeks, in self-disgust. 'I bloody-well *knew* it! Play silly buggers with Henry Collins, and this happens. You dunno which way you're facing. You dunno whether you're coming or going. Why the hell didn't you find another copper, Henry? Why had it to be *me*?'

'I trust you,' said Collins, simply.

Lennox finished the sandwich he was chewing his way through, de-coked his gullet with a long swig of strong sweet tea, then took a cellophane-wrapped cheroot from a breast-pocket of the hacking-jacket, stripped it and held it between his lips.

As he struck a match, and held the flame to the tobacco-leaf, he said, 'You have to win, mate. I'm clobbered. If that's the way you want it ... off the record.'

*They called them bombers' moons. The lunatics to whom war was still a semi-romantic, man-to-man affair – the arm-chair warriors, and the factory hands who laughed at canteen jokes told on 'Workers' Playtime' – called them bombers' moons. There was even a film, called 'Bombers' Moon'.*

*A nice phrase. As neat a way of wrapping terror in pink ribbons as you could wish for.*

*And there it was. Massive and silver, surrounded by its cortège of stars, and flooding the snow-capped peaks and the waters of the fiord with light as white as death itself. Not a cloud – not so much as a whisp – and, fifteen thousand feet below, Trondheim ... and the U-boat pens.*

*In this light, it was even possible to see the occasional Lanc, hauling its bomb-load towards the target.*

*The voice of the master-bomber.*

*'Keep coming, main force. We're marking the target, now.'*

*Crowe couldn't see the markers go down, ahead of them, but he knew what they'd look like. Explosions of pillar-box red. Two – maybe three – and the master-bomber would recce, decide which marker was nearest to the target, then bring in the main bombing force.*

*Meanwhile . . .*

*You tightened your gut muscles, and your jaw muscles.
You started the sweating-it-out period. Sometimes, you sent
a quick prayer to your Maker . . . 'Just this once. Just let me
get away with it – just this once – and I'll never ever kill
women and kids again.'*

*Collins's voice over the intercom.*

*'Gunners. Watch out for fighters.'*

*Ray's voice, 'Bomb doors open, skipper.'*

*'Thank you, bomb-aimer.'*

*Then, nothing other than the noise. The noise you'd
grown accustomed to over the last few hours. Noise and
movement. The pounding roar of the engines. The rush of
the slipstream. The continual shudder of the Lanc itself
as it pushed its way forward and now and then bucked
a little as it hit an air pocket or caught the back-lash of
another slipstream.*

*Crowe flicked the intercom switch on his oxygen mask,
and called, 'Fighter coming in, skipper. From the rear.
Port quarter . . . one o'clock.'*

*'Thanks, Jimmy. No evasive action. He's all yours.'*

*Alf's voice, saying, 'Okay, Jimmy. I have him.'*

*Crowe leaned forward, and stared through the dull glow
of the ring and bead of the reflector sight. Waiting for the
wing-span to fill the ring. An M.E. . . . so much like a Hurri-
cane, it had to be an M.E. Overtaking from the light half
of the sky . . . damn near silhouetted against that full moon.
A mug. A square-headed twit. The boys who knew their
onions came at you from the dark half of the sky . . . they
silhouetted you against whatever light was going.*

*Ray's voice saying, 'Flack ahead, skipper.'*

*'Check. How's it going with the fighter, Jimmy?'*

*'He's coming in. We have him.'*

*Alf's voice, saying, 'Stand by for a coconut.'*

126

*A mug. A square-headed twit. A rule-book merchant. Overtaking speed ... thirty. The book says so. Any faster, and you can't get a long enough burst. Any slower, and you're a sitting target. Thirty – then peel away to port ... and that gives Alf a beautiful, raking burst, right along the length of your belly.*

*Sweetheart, whoever taught you never fought a Lancaster. Never tangled with a Lanc whose gunners had seen him first. Come on, sweetheart – just those few yards nearer ... you're about to die for your fatherland.*

*Battle range ... six hundred yards. Six hundred yards, you square-headed twit. That's when we start scrapping. Six guns – four here, and two in the mid-upper – and each muzzle spewing out fifteen hundred rounds a minute. Every fifth a tracer. Every fifth armour-piercing. Every fifth ex-plosive. And all the rest .303 ball ammo. Nine-thousand wasps a minute, sweetheart ... and every one with a sting in its tail. And all six guns were lined-up, this very morning; lined up, on a single black dot, six hundred yards away. That's what's waiting for you, sweetheart. That's the size of the frog you're due to catch in your stupid throat.*

Alf's voice, saying, 'I make it eight hundred, and he's started firing.'

'Seven-fifty. Let him come. He's wasting ammo.'

*The hell he's wasting ammo!*

Something plucked at Crowe's sleeve, and almost jerked his hand from the trigger-bar.

'Let him have it, Alf. Let him ride into the bloody stuff.'

Crowe squeezed both hands on the trigger-bar, eased the guns and the Frazer-Nash turret, to keep the M.E. plumb in the ring of the sight. The servo-feed lifted the four belts of bullets, from the entrance hole in the base of the turret, to the breeches of the four guns. The four cocking-levers flew, backwards and forwards, at a speed the eye couldn't follow.

The catch-trays caught the empty cartridges, as they were ejected, and fed them into the chute, to be cascaded out and into the slipstream.

Crowe could feel the shudder of the trigger-bar as the guns fired, in quadruple unison. He could see the four paths of red tracer – every fifth bullet – as they converged on the oncoming Messerschmitt. He could even smell a whiff of cordite, on the air, as it filtered into his oxygen mask.

But he could hear nothing, above the blasting roar of the four engines which hauled the Lanc towards its target, and the rush of the slipstream as the giant plane tore a passage through the air.

The wisdom of the grizzled gunnery instructor rattled through his brain, like a badly threaded cinematograph film.

'Never mind the fancy theories, lads ... You're not buying the bullets ... Forget bullet-trail ... Forget speed-allowance ... When it happens, you haven't time for arithmetic ... Stick the bead on the spinner, and keep it there ... Five-second bursts, then your guns won't jam ... Bead on the spinner, and you'll be hitting him, before he's hitting you.'

But it wasn't happening. IT WASN'T HAPPENING!

The dark outline of the M.E. was growing bigger – getting nearer – against the lighter darkness of the sky. And bullets were being exchanged for bullets. Hundreds of bullets. Thousands of bullets. British bullets and German bullets. A gun-fight of monumental proportions ... the expression 'shooting war' reduced to a terrifying man-versus-man reality.

Crowe muttered, 'Fly into it, you bastard. Fly into it!'

And then, it happened.

Tiny pieces of the M.E. were being nibbled away. Along the wings. On the tail fin. Nibbles – bites – like a hungry mouse nibbling at cheese.

The M.E. wobbled, then righted itself ... then came on,

*like a drunken fighter, refusing to accept defeat, even when
he's out on his feet.*

*The Brownings still vibrated the trigger-bar. The tracers
were punching home and, with them, four times as many
other rounds. The M.E. seemed to flutter, under the pounding, then wheeled to port and tried to climb. Crowe followed
the wheel and climb with the reflector sight, and kept his
fingers hard on the triggers. From the corner of his eye he
saw twin streams of tracer from the mid-upper turret, peck-
ing at the dying Messerschmitt.*

*Then, almost as it turned to run for safety, the fighter
seemed to crumble and fall, like a broken moth. No ex-
plosion. No flames. Nothing spectacular. Just the shattered
death of a fighting machine, and the unknown man who'd
controlled it.*

*From the astrodome Junior let out an Indian war-whoop
of delight.*

*Crowe said, 'He's going down, skipper,' and his voice
was dry and harsh.*

*'Thanks, gunners. Good show.'*

*Then, Ray's voice saying, 'Flack's getting heavier, skipper.
Unusual, too.'*

*'Check. Watch for the markers.'*

*The voice of the master-bomber.*

*'Stand easy, main force. Master-bomber to main force.
Stand easy. I repeat – stand easy.'*

Collins smoked a cigarette in his briar holder, and said,
'Emmerson. How is he?'

'Smashed up a bit. Skull damage. Concussion . . . the usual
thing.'

'Critical?'

'He'll live,' grunted Lennox, and swigged tea from his
mug.

'He has a son. Peter.'

'Aye. We haven't been able to contact him, yet.'

'No-o,' said Collins, gently. 'You wouldn't.'

'What's that mean?' Lennox's protruding eyes took on a look of suspicious interest.

'Tell me, Lenny,' said Collins, 'do you do football pools?'

'Eh?'

'Football pools. Homes, draws and aways. You put crosses, and ...'

'I know what football pools are, mate. I just don't see ...'

'Do you fill them in.'

'Well – since you ask – no. I don't even *like* the game.'

'Emmerson did,' drawled Collins.

'I don't give a damn what Emmerson liked. As far as I'm ...'

'No ... I mean he filled in football pools.'

'That,' snorted Lennox, 'has made my day. To know that Emmerson filled in football pools, is summat I've always wanted...'

'He won thirty-two-thousand pounds, last week,' said Collins in a soft, unemotional voice. 'And *now*, you can't find his son.'

'I don't see the ...' Lennox stopped, blinked, then said, 'Yes, by Christ, I *do*.'

'It had to come,' said Collins, sadly. '*Somebody* had to think of it.'

'You're sure?' It wasn't a real doubt ... more of a verification.

'That's why James is here.'

'James?'

'Crowe.'

'Oh!'

'The usual thing. Don't tell the police. He didn't ... he told his brother-in-law. And *he* came to me for help.'

'Hence the off-the-record lark?'

'Quite.'

Lennox puffed his cheroot, meditatively, then rumbled, 'But you *have* told the cops, old cock. You've told *me*, and I'm a ...'

'You're a valued friend. The sort of friend who doesn't betray confidences.'

'Now, lookee ...'

'Who gives his word ... and then keeps it.'

'Henry, old squire.' Lennox pushed back his chair and prowled the room as he talked. He scowled, and smoked the evil-smelling cheroot ... waving it, periodically, whenever he wanted to emphasise a point. He said, 'I'm big stuff these days. Detective chief superintendent. Head of C.I.D. ... no less. I dunno who the hell pulled my name out of the hat. I don't much care. It's a good job, and I enjoy it. And why do I enjoy it, Henry? Do I have to tell *you?* Because being a copper means something. To me ... like it did to you. Okay – I'm not like you ... not like you *were*. I'm rough. Rough as a bear's arse ... but I know it, and it's my way of bobbying. They laugh at me. Don't tell me – I know ... when a bloke looks like me, what else can he do? I'm a joke, Henry ... but I'm *not* a bloody joke. I let 'em laugh – I even encourage 'em to laugh ... 'cos, while they're laughing they ain't *looking*. They laugh, tears come to their eyes, they can't see ... and that's when I've *got* 'em. Cops, as well as comedians.

'But – y'know – some of the coppers *don't* laugh. They don't laugh, because they don't like me. They hate my guts ... which means they've a big enough area to hate, and they have a birthday. I'm what they should be ... get it? I'm wearing *their* shoes. *Their* rank. I'm sitting on *their* chair, in *their* office. And, give 'em half a chance, and they'll have me ... and enjoy it. So-o ... if I sit on a known crime.

Especially one the size of kidnapping. Henry, old cock, I'm opening my collar, to give 'em an uninterrupted view of my throat ... ain't I?'

'Indeed.' Collins nodded sage agreement.

Lennox continued his pacing.

He rumbled, 'All right. Why the hell should I?'

'Why, indeed?'

'You conned the agreement out of me. You can't deny that.'

'A certain amount of mild conning,' agreed Collins.

'And a promise, made on the strength of a con ... what's it worth?'

'Very little.'

'I was sucked in ... that's about the strength of it.'

'Possibly,' murmured Collins. 'Possibly.'

'I mean, dammit all ...' Lennox waved the cheroot, wildly. Kidnapping! It ain't like nicking milk bottles.'

'Indeed, it isn't.'

'I could end up behind bars *myself*, if I sat on summat that size.'

'You could,' agreed Collins.

'You, too, old cock. You could be there, with me.'

'How, precisely?' asked Collins, with interest. 'Why?'

'For covering up crime, for Christ's sake.'

'Me?'

'As a citizen. You have duties, as a citizen, Henry ... don't kid me you don't know *that*. And, failing to report a kidnapping is ...'

'Which kidnapping?' Collins's expression was one of mild, but taunting, mockery.

'Emmerson's son. You've just told me ...'

'That Emmerson won some money on a football pool. That's all, Lenny. *You* told *me* his son's missing ... remember? That you haven't been able to contact him. And, as for *kidnapping* ... that word hasn't passed my lips.'

It stopped Lennox in his tracks. Even Lennox. The fat detective chief superintendent froze in a stance of sheer disbelief; his cheroot part-way to his mouth, his head turned towards Collins, his feet motionless after their last stride.

The tableau lasted all of fifteen seconds.

Then, Collins smiled, and said, 'Well?'

'I could – I could ask Emmerson,' croaked Lennox.

'He'd tell you nothing.'

'The hell he would. It's his kid who's ...'

'Who'll die, if he opens his mouth to the police.'

'All right. Your pal, Crowe. I could ask him.'

'Like me, he knows very little ... and, you have my assurance, he'll tell you less.'

'All right. I could start the enquiry ... on an *assumption*.'

'And,' said Collins, in a flat voice, 'when you dig up young Emmerson, you could live with your conscience ... could you?'

Lennox moved. He moved like a man suddenly grown old; he lowered his bulk back onto the chair, enjoyed the doubtful luxury of a sigh which started at the soles of his socks, then shook his head in slow defeat.

He growled, 'That's the barrel I'm over, is it? Official ... and the kid pays with his life?'

'We've had the warning. We'd be wise to believe it.'

'So-o, it really *is* "off the record"? It *has* to be?'

'Were I in your shoes ...' began Collins, then stopped.

'C'mon,' said Lennox, heavily. 'My shoes ... what would *you* do?'

'We know things,' said Collins, gently. 'I *still* know things. Every police officer who works his area of responsibility – beat, section, division, even force area – *knows* things. Often, he knows far more about crime he can't prove than he does about crime he can prove. If he has any sense, he keeps quiet ... and waits. He waits for the wrong move ... for the moment when he *can* prove. Then, the chickens come home to roost, and the villains wonder why. They wonder how it was done. They wonder why they've become vulnerable. The old saw – "a little knowledge" – it can, indeed, be a dangerous thing ... for the wrongdoer, and in the hands of a police officer who knows the meaning of patience.'

'You're a good lad, Henry old cock,' said Lennox, wrily. 'I take that as a compliment.'

'Good enough to tell *this* grandmother how to suck eggs.' Collins smiled.

'So-o, we'll do it your way. Strictly under the table.'

'Wise,' murmured Collins.

Lennox dragged on his cheroot, and said, 'Tell me what you know, squire. Everything you know ... if it's lifting the crown jewels, I'll still sit on it.'


*'Stand easy, main force. Master-bomber to main force. Stand easy. I repeat – stand easy.'*

*Alf's voice said, 'That flack. It's "flaming onions". World War One stuff. My old man told me about it.'*

*It was, too. Some red, some green. Curling up, in a slight bow, from fifteen thousand feet below. Slowly. Lazily. For all the world like a string of burning beads. But, as the beads reached their height they increased speed ... and, suddenly, they weren't beads. They were anti-aircraft shells. Deadly, and a hell of a lot of 'em. And a hell of a lot of the conventional stuff mixed among.*

*Crowe kept his voice calm, as he said, 'I think I've stopped one in the left arm, skipper. Left forearm.'*

*'Bad?'*

*'No – a fair amount of blood ... but it's still usable.'*

*'No heroics, Jim.'*

134

'It's okay, skip. Just reporting ... that's all.'

'Fine. Stick it, till we've unloaded the bombs. Then, come up front, and we'll fix it.'

Ray's voice said, 'Skipper, shouldn't we ...'

'Quiet, crew. No unnecessary chat.'

And now, the flack was getting rough. Really rough. They'd more than a few guns down there, and they were popping them off like crazy. The Lanc shuddered and bucked as the shells burst ahead, to port, to starboard and behind the tail. Bucked and jerked, like a frightened animal, with its port wing lowered as Collins circled the target and waited for more orders from the master-bomber.

And the searchlights. White beams – like the beams from some ogre's torch – fanning the sky, in an attempt to pinpoint gnats in the darkness. White beams ... thank God not those beams with the neon-blue tinge. The neon-blue beams didn't have to search – they knew ... they were radar-controlled. From a blip on a screen, they nailed an aircraft as easily, and as certainly, as putting a key in a lock. Then the white beams – the manually operated beams – swung in, and coned ... and, from then on, the gunners had a specific aiming-point. They could see the gnat!

But, this time, the neon-blue beams were missing. Maybe there was a technical reason. Maybe the radar beams were strictly for German soil. Maybe anything – but, thank God ... the white beams were groping around the sky and finding nothing.

Fifteen minutes ... thereabouts.

It felt like fifteen years; fifteen years of prolonged stomach-cramp.

Crowe saw a peak and a shore-line slide from under the turret for the fourth – maybe fifth – time.

He said, 'Rear turret to skipper.'

'Go ahead, Jim.'

135

'What the hell are we hanging around here for, skipper?'
'You heard the master-bomber.'
'Yeah ... abort mission. Return to base.'
'"Stand easy". The code word for orbit target.'
'Sorry, skipper. Orbit target ... code word "Attention".'
'You've made a mistake, James. It's ...'
'You've made the mistake. "Attention" ... orbit target
and wait for further orders. "Stand easy" ... abandon mis-
sion and return to base.'

Alf's voice said, 'Christ! That was twenty minutes back.
No wonder it's getting rough. We're the only bloody kite
left for 'em to aim at.'

'Quiet, crew.' Collins paused, then said, 'I'm flashing
Mac. He has it in black and white.'

Mac's voice came over the intercom, 'Skipper? Wireless-
op here.'

'Code words?' asked Collins.

'Sure. "Attention", orbit target. "Stand easy", return
to base.'

'Holy cow! Let's get the hell out of here.'

'Cool down, Alf. We're on our ...'

A giant hand seemed to grab the Lanc. The hand
squeezed, then shook the plane till every rivet threatened
to pop from its socket. Then the hand opened its fingers,
and they weren't flying straight and level any more.

Crowe saw the moon-washed landscape tilt, slide to starboard then disappear from view. He saw a star-sprinkled
sky ahead of his turret and felt the drag as the plane shook
and raced its way, nose first, towards the waters of the fiord.
There was a great wind, and a great noise ... and the gabble
over the intercom told its own terrifying story.

Then, Collins shouted. He actually shouted through the
intercom ... which, in itself, shocked everybody into a state
of near-calm.

136

'*PILOT TO CREW. EVERY CREW MEMBER STAYS AT HIS POST. EVERY CREW MEMBER KEEPS HIS MOUTH SHUT, UNLESS HE ANSWERS A QUESTION FROM ME.*'

*Then, silence, except for the great rush of wind and the groan and creak of the airframe, as it took a strain it was never built to take.*

*And gradually – oh, so gradually – the landscape came back into view from under Crowe's feet, and the old Lanc was straight and level again. But low ... my God, how low! The flack and the flaming onions were way and gone to hell, upstairs. At this height, the anti-aircraft boys didn't need flack ... they could damn near prod the Lanc with bayonets.*

*But, the old girl still flew. With shudders and aerodynamic hiccups guaranteed to make your hair curl ... but the old bastard was still airborne.*

*Collins said, 'Engineer. A quick run-down on damage, please.'*

*'Port outer's gone. Starboard inner's on its last legs ... I think it was on fire, before the dive. And starboard outer ... that's coughing like an old man. Port inner seems okay. I don't think we've lost any juice, and the hydraulics and the electrical circuits don't seem to be damaged. There's a few holes, here and there ... fusilage, mainly. That's about all, skipper.'*

*'Bomb-aimer?'*

*'Half the Perspex in the nose isn't there any more. The bomb-sight's been buckled. Other than that, okay.'*

*'And you?'*

*'I think I caught a few bruises on the way down ... that's all.'*

*'Mid-upper?'*

*'Okay, skipper. I can see a few holes, here and there ...*

137

and, with luck, my guts should soon catch up with the rest of me.'

'Navigator?'

'A couple of broken pencils, and I've lost my maps. Other than that, okay.'

'Wireless-op?'

'Fine, skipper. The cat's whisker's still working.'

'Good. Rear-gunner?'

'Okay, skipper. I'm still with you.'

'And the arm?'

'Still bleeding ... but, that's okay.'

Collins handled the Lanc. He didn't fly it, he fought it; he dragged its wounded and quivering bulk around the bends, between the mountains flanking the fiord and, every second, they lost a little more height.

The crew stayed quiet. They couldn't help ... those who believed in prayer, could only pray.

They reached the open sea and, in a slow, bone-shaking turn, the Lanc swung to port and pointed its nose for home.

Then, the starboard inner gave up the ghost and, a couple of minutes later, its twin, the starboard outer died.

Then, Collins spoke.

'Your attention, please, gentlemen.' He sounded like a director at a meeting of shareholders. Calm. Unhurried. Panting a little, from his exertions but, other than that, quite confident. 'The situation. These beauties can fly on one engine. We all know that ... we all had a demonstration at Op Training Unit. They won't climb and, in rarefied atmosphere, they gradually lose height. But, give them dense enough air, and they'll hold their own. That's why we're going down to zero feet. We're going to wave-hop our way back. Ray – Jim – Alf ... come out of your turrets. Make yourselves as comfortable as possible in the main body. Jim

138

– get that arm seen to. Junior – keep your eye on the fuel
... balance the tanks out, as much as you can, to counter the
starboard drag. Mac – keep listening out, and be ready
to send out a fix if things get nasty. Johnny – course for
the nearest U.K. landfall ... and keep checking. And – all
of you – fingers crossed, and be ready for dinghy positions,
in case we're forced to land in the hog. Everybody got
that?'

It was the journey of a lifetime. The flight of a lifetime
... and, never-ending. The whitecaps of the Atlantic were
there ... damn near within touching distance. And cold
... and every man knew that, fix or no fix, the Air-Sea-
Rescue boys wouldn't have a cat in hell's chance of finding
them in that expanse of ocean.

Sweden, as neutral ground upon which to land, was out.
Until they were well south of Bergen, the peaks between
Norway and Sweden pushed upwards to three thousand
feet ... and the crippled Lanc couldn't make that height.
And, south of Bergen, home-base wasn't much farther than
Sweden, anyway.

The choice was simple ... U.K., or the drink.

They made it – ruptured-duck fashion – and with the
twelve-hundred-pounder still tucked away in the bomb-bay.
To jetison that egg, at zero feet, would certainly have landed
them in Norway ... all over Norway!

It wasn't so much a flight home. It was more of a prolonged all-in wrestling match, between a four-engined
bomber and its pilot. But the pilot won, and his one-engine
landing was a mite raggy but, nevertheless, a thing of pure
inspiration, and he rolled the battered old Lanc round the
perimeter track, and he tucked it neatly in position alongside the hut at the dispersal point, and then he cut the single
engine which had hauled them home.

He looked up at Junior, and gasped, 'Fuel?'

*Junior grinned, and said, 'We've some left, skipper ...
just about enough to fill a lighter.'*

*And then Collins collapsed forward, over the column.*

*Later that day – when they'd slept, and awakened, and
were sprucing themselves up for an evening in Lincoln –
Collins walked into the crew hut ... to* apologise, *of all
things!*

*He blamed himself. He shouldn't have goofed on the code
words.*

*Alf said, 'You did it the hard way, skipper.'*

*'What?' Collins raised an enquiring smile on his grey and
tired face.*

*'We could have made the drink. In the fiord. Got ashore
... and the Norwegians are on our side, y'know.'*

*'P.O.W.?' asked Collins.*

*'Possibly ... but, from what I hear, it's not unbearable.'*

*Collins said, 'Are you a fight fan, Alf?'*

*Alf looked puzzled, raised a shoulder, then said, 'Yeah ...
I suppose.'*

*'The first Louis–Schmelling fight?'*

*'Uhuh. What of it?'*

*'Hitler – if you recall – made Schmelling a hero, for
demonstrating the supremacy of the white race ... until
Louis dislocated Schmelling's spine, with a punch to the
ribs, in the return fight. Hitler didn't like that.'*

*'Oh!'*

*'You see what I'm getting at, gentlemen?' Collins eyed
his crew, quizzically. 'If it's possible, at all, Jimmy isn't
going to pay for Schmelling's dislocated spine.'*

In an odd way, Lennox resembled a down-in-the-mouth,
bald-headed panda; he looked cuddly, but inconsolable.
Alternatively, he looked like an over-weight Buddha, with
gut-rot.

'Bloody champion,' he muttered, gloomily. 'A daylight snatch. Emmerson daren't say a word. Your pal, out there, gets the hump. The only nerk we might have screwed a lead from is stiffening, on a slab. And you're the Jack-The-Lad who's spreadeagled me in the fertiliser with all the "off-the-record" chat. We're up a gum tree, old cock. We ain't even got a starting point.'

Collins kept a straight face, and waited.

'I mean ... what the deuce?' grumbled Lennox. 'I ask Emmerson a few pointed questions and, if you're right, he'll tell me to shove my head in the nearest oven.'

'That, he will,' agreed Collins.

'All right ... but *why*?'

'His son's life depends on it.'

'His son's life depends on somebody *doing* something.'

'Or the ransom.'

'Henry! They won't ... they hardly ever *do*.'

'I know ... hardly ever.'

'So, why the blazes can't he trust us?'

'Skin colour,' said Collins, sadly.

'In God's name, what difference does *that* make?'

'None to you. None to me. All the difference in the world, to *him*.'

'There's no sense – there's no gumption ...'

'You won't alter it, Lenny. It's too deep-rooted for one generation to wipe out.'

'Your pal, Crowe ...' began Lennox.

'Given time, I can talk him round.'

'We don't *have* much time.'

'I know.'

'If that kid's been lifted ...'

'He has.'

'... and if it ain't a one-man job. Hicks.'

'Stop wishing for the moon, Lenny.'

'All right. If Hicks is in with 'em.'

'He *must* be. Otherwise, why kill Davenport? Otherwise, why was Emmerson driving the vehicle?'

'The chances are,' agreed Lennox, heavily.

The two men were engrossed in their conversation. They didn't notice the door of the study open.

Lennox rumbled, 'If the bastards who've lifted him get to know about his father being in police hands ...'

'The chances are they *already* know.'

'... they'll never believe he hasn't told us about his son.'

'They will,' said Collins, with some confidence.

'Come on, Henry! They ain't gonna ...'

'It's part of Hicks's death. Part of the accident. They'll reconstruct it, the same way we've reconstructed it.'

'I wouldn't bet shirt buttons on it, mate.'

'They'll believe,' said Collins, firmly, 'because we'll *make* them believe. What the police don't know, the police can't even hint at. And the police *don't* know officially.'

'Christ, we're back to that, again.'

'It's our only real hope. To let things run their course ... let them feel secure enough not to kill the boy.'

A voice said, 'What's the plan of action, skipper?'

Crowe was standing at the open door.

He half-smiled his embarrassment at Lennox, then said, 'I ain't the best in the world at apologising, Mr Lennox.'

'Lenny to my friends.' Lennox gave a wry smile, and added, 'Why not join the few I have?'

'Okay, Lenny. And – *y'know* ... sorry for blowing steam.'

The wry smile widened into a pumpkin grin, and Lennox said, 'I've a hide, old cock. Cats sharpen their claws on it ... not to mention the missus.'

'And, finally,' said Miss Benson, looking up from her spiral-backed notebook, 'there's the question of the boy, Emmerson – Peter Emmerson ... I've made a note, in case you had anything in mind.'

'Ah, yes, Emmerson.' Adams tapped a soft tattoo on the desk top with the tips of his right fingers. His face creased into an expression of academic annoyance. 'I – er – I heard the news, about his father, on the radio. While I was shaving. It – er – it poses a problem, I think.'

'He has no other next-of-kin ... as I understand things.'

'Quite.'

'Which makes us – the school, I mean ...' She paused, then said, 'More or less *in loco parentis*.'

'Throughout the school day, we're always *that*, Miss Benson,' said Adams, primly.

'Yes, headmaster. But – I mean ... after school hours?'

Adams drummed a desk-top tattoo for a few more moments, then said, 'I think I'll have a word with him. Find which class he's in, and ...'

'He hasn't reported in, this morning, sir.'

'What?'

'I checked. He's absent. He hasn't been back since that silly prank, yesterday morning.'

'Oh, dear.' Adams sighed, and ran worried fingers through his prematurely grey hair. 'Modern youth, Miss Benson. One can rely upon them for only one thing ... to be *un*reliable.'

'He's – er – he's probably very worried about his father.'

'Naturally.'

'It's where he might be,' suggested Miss Benson.

'Where?'

'The City Hospital. With his father.'

'Where his father was supposed to have been yesterday,' said Adams, irritably. He sighed, again, then said, 'Yes ... I suppose you're right.'

'He shouldn't be left there, sir.'

Adams looked up at her, and said, 'If you have some suggestion you wish to make, Miss Benson ...' and waited.

She cleared her throat, then said, 'At lunch time, headmaster – with your permission, of course – I could go to the hospital.'

Adams raised his eyebrows and nodded, slowly.

Encouraged, Miss Benson said, 'If the boy's there – *assuming* he's there, that is – I could bring him back to school. I could enquire from his father ... what – er – course he'd prefer us to take.'

'Assuming the police allow you access to Emmerson.'

'Well – er – yes ... assuming that, of course. But I think they will. For the sake of the boy.'

Adams mulled over the suggestion for a moment, or two, then said, 'We have a responsibility towards the boy, I suppose.'

'I think so, headmaster.'

'In the absence of any close kin.'

'Yes, sir.'

'Ye-es.' Adams allowed a scholarly smile, then said, 'I think *my* presence might add weight, Miss Benson. As a means of offsetting any objections the police might have, I mean. I think we'll both go ... shall we say, in an hour's time? At ten-thirty? Will that be convenient?'

'Yes, headmaster. Quite convenient.'

'Good ... you might let the deputy head know, please.'

'Yes, sir.'

'And, if you'll be here, in my office, in an hour.'

Lipton, the taxi-firm proprietor, felt a mite foolish. This 'statement' business might be the ultra-modern way of coppering, but it was far too clinical for *his* liking.

That smart-Alick jack – what was his name? ... Joyce. Joyce had dumped him in this glorified telephone booth, pointed to the hand-mike, recited the instructions (instructions which were, anyway, printed on a framed card, on the wall, in kindergarten language) and then hoofed it off to some other corner of this rambling nick.

And, here he was, holding the hand-mike, like an electronic ice-cream cornet ... having (as per instructions) given his full name, his age, his occupation, his address and the present times and date ... and not knowing what the hell to say (as per further instructions) when it came to the bit that read ...

GIVE YOUR STATEMENT IN YOUR OWN WORDS. SPEAK AT A NORMAL SPEED. BE AS CHRONOLOGICALLY ACCURATE AS POSSIBLE. INCLUDE ONLY RELEVANT DETAILS. AT THE END OF YOUR STATEMENT GIVE THE TIME AND DATE. REPLACE THE MICROPHONE ON ITS REST, AND THE MACHINE WILL AUTOMATICALLY CEASE RECORDING.

Big deal!

So where did the rates and taxes go? To pay for gimmicks like this? Do-it-yourself bobbying, for Christ's sake?

Lipton cleared his throat, and launched into statement-making.

'It was yesterday. That would be Monday, the twenty-

145

sixth. At just after eleven. In the morning, that is. We got this call phoned in. To City Taxis ... that's my firm. Sorry! Sorry! Just *before* eleven ... not just after. Ten to eleven. Ten minutes to eleven. That's when it was booked in. A call from somebody called Chambers – a man – to send a taxi to fifteen Fairfax Avenue. Right away. To take him to the bus depot. So, I sent Garfield. Leonard Garfield ... that's his full name. He'd just shown into the office, and he was handy. So he's the one I sent. He took one of the taxis. A Morris 1100. Black saloon. UGX.9986.T ... that's its registration number. And that's the last time I saw the bl ... The last time I saw the car. Garfield did the Fairfax Avenue job. Then he called in to ask if there was anything else, and there was. We'd just had a call from Gladstone Comprehensive School. To take some kid to the City Hospital. A kid called Emmerson. So I sent Garfield on to the school, to pick up this kid, and that's the last time we heard from him. Then, when it got to about two o'clock – in the afternoon, that is – and we hadn't heard from Garfield, I decided to telephone the police, and tell them. The car was missing, see? The taxi. And he hadn't called in. So I thought I'd better ......'

The farm truck rattled and bounced its way along the dirt road, like an exaggerated mock-up for a shoe-string production of Steinbeck's *Grapes of Wrath*. It had started life as a Ford but, at this moment, the Ford people would have happily disowned it; throughout its long, working life it had collected bits and pieces from just about every other make of automobile under the sun, and every bit and every piece had had to be bashed and cut into an approximate shape, before it had been welded into position. It was as ugly as a camel ... and as stubborn as a drunken mule.

Garfield fought the wheel. There was damn near twelve

146

inches of play, and the tyre pressures (or something) didn't match and (like they do in old-fashioned movies) he had to saw the wheel, left-right-left-right, to keep the truck on a more, or less, straight path. At the corners, he dropped down to second, in order to coax it into the direction he wanted it to take.

The youth said, 'Where are we going, Mr Garfield?'

'Skip it, Pete.' Garfield held his concentration on the road ahead. 'I can't talk and drive this bloody contraption, at the same time.'

The youth asked no more questions.

The youth's wrists were tied behind his back, with bright orange, nylon, baler-twine. His ankles were lashed together with the same sort of twine. It was strong, and it didn't stretch and, just to be sure, a triple-loop of twine linked his left arm to the tubular steel of the bucket-seat on which he sat. He was neither blindfolded, nor gagged and, twice, he'd seen sign-posts with their fingers pointing towards villages he'd never heard of.

The track snaked its way along the slope of a hill – a small mountain – with its twin closing towards them, or receding away from them, across the uneven sweep of the valley. A river played hide-and-seek with sheep-grazing land, and rock outcrops, along the floor of the valley and, on all sides, peaks humped their bracken-laced backs towards the rain-heavy sky; peaks whose names were High Ruckles and Hambleton Hill, Meugher and Rain Stang ... and the river which flowed along the floor of the valley was the River Nidd.

But the youth didn't know these things.

The youth was lost ... and the youth was beginning to feel genuinely frightened.

The uniformed police constable, on duty in the corridor, by the door of the tiny, one-bed ward, did his job as he'd been ordered to do it. Politely, but firmly.

He said, 'I'm sorry, sir. Hospital and police personnel, only.'

'I'm his headmaster,' said Adams.

'Yes, sir.'

'I'm interested in the welfare of his son. That's all I want to see him about.'

'Yes, sir,' repeated the constable. 'But ... I'm still sorry.'

Miss Benson said, 'All right. If we can't see Mr Emmerson, can you help us?'

'In what way, ma'am?'

'Miss.'

'Sorry, miss ... in what way?'

'Well, tell us where the boy is,' said Adams. 'What's going to happen to *him*?'

'I dunno, sir. I've got this job. I've been told to do it. They don't keep me up to date with things.'

'Has he been here?' asked Miss Benson.

'Who's that, miss?'

'The boy – Peter Emmerson ... has he been to see his father?'

'Not since I arrived.'

'And, how long's that since?' asked Adams.

'I came with Emmerson from the operating room.'

'So he *hasn't* been?'

The P.C. said, 'Not here, sir. Maybe at Out-Patients. Maybe at the Enquiry Desk. But, not here.'

148

Adams looked annoyed, and snapped, 'Look, officer, that boy ...'

'I'm sorry, sir.' The constable didn't like being snapped at. 'I get my orders. I obey 'em. Hospital personnel, and police ...'

The constable drew himself up to attention, and said, 'Good morning, sir,' as Lennox and the coloured man made the trio into a quintet.

Adams turned to Lennox, and said, 'Ah! You're – er ...' He paused, swallowed as his brain took in the hacking-jacket, pullover and trousers then, in a slightly dumb-founded tone, completed his question. 'You're in charge, are you?'

'D'you have a reason for wanting to know?' countered Lennox.

'I – er – yes. I'd like a few words with Emmerson.'

Lennox shook his head, with great solemnity.

'Why not?' asked Adams.

'Unless you've a thumping good reason.'

'I'd like to speak to him about his son.'

'Oh, aye?' Lennox proved the argument that any good copper can work rings round any Oscar winner, by keeping a slightly gormless expression pinned firmly in place. He said, 'What about his son?'

'I'm the headmaster of the school – Gladstone Comprehensive – of which the boy's a pupil. As I understand it, the boy – Peter Emmerson – has no next-of-kin, and I'm making some ...'

'Oh, but he has,' interrupted Lennox.

'What?'

'Relatives. This is his uncle.' Lennox jerked his head towards Crowe. 'He's here to make arrangements about the boy.'

'Oh! I – er – I wasn't aware ...'

'Good of you, though,' said Lennox.

Adams turned to Crowe, and said, 'Please see the boy returns to school as soon as possible, Mr – er ...'

'Crowe,' said Crowe.

'I realise he must be distressed. But the sooner he returns to some semblance of normality the better.'

'I'll make sure he gets back to his schooling, as soon as he can,' promised Crowe ... and meant it.

Miss Benson murmured, 'And, if there's anything we can do – anything at all ...'

'Thank you, ma'am.'

'Miss.'

'Thank you, miss,' Crowe corrected himself.

Lennox spoke to the constable.

He said, 'Who's in there, with him?'

'Detective Sergeant Ingram, sir.'

'Fine. Nip in, son. Tell Ingram to knock off for a few minutes – take a break for coffee, or summat ... and let Mr Crowe have about fifteen minutes with his brother-in-law. In private. Okay?'

'Yes, sir.'

The constable looked slightly taken aback but, when detective chief superintendents hold a hoop at the ready, common or garden coppers don't hesitate ... they do the hoop-jumping trick, without question.

The constable disappeared into the tiny ward.

Lennox eased Adams and Benson along the corridor, and towards the exit. He shepherded them gently, and without fuss, and (a trick of the trade of policing) without them being consciously aware of the fact that they were being shepherded. And, all the time, he kept up a continuous flow of unimportant conversation.

'Good of you to come, headmaster. Good of you to spare a thought for the lad.'

'Not at all. We have a responsibility.'

'Anyway, Crowe'll see to things now.'

'I take it the boy will remain a pupil of Gladstone Comprehensive?'

'I reckon ... at least, till things sort themselves out.'

'Mr Crowe? He lives in Bordfield?'

'No ... Liverpool, actually.'

'In that case ...'

'As I understand it, he's gonna hang on here, till after the trial.'

'Oh! Of course ... that's quite natural.'

'So-o, the lad'll still attend Gladstone.'

Miss Benson said, 'We'll do our best to shield him from publicity, of course.'

'Good of you, miss,' rumbled Lennox.

'It's likely to be difficult,' said Adams, sadly. 'The whole school – I need hardly go into the finer details ...'

'We'll have a word with the press boys,' promised Lennox.

'I'm obliged.'

'And there's some good neighbours in Christopher Crescent ... they'll chase the nosey types away, after school hours.'

'Good. I'm pleased.'

'We'll see to the lad.' Lennox smiled a smile which was tinged with sadness. 'The sins o' the fathers – y'know ... we do our best to make sure they ain't visited upon their sons.'

That was the brand of talk which passed between Lennox, Adams and Benson and, in no time at all, they reached Adams's car, they shook hands and Adams and Benson drove off, towards Gladstone Comprehensive School.

Lennox waddled across the parking lot, climbed into

his ancient Alvis and, in turn, drove back to Bordfield
Regional Metropolitan Police District Headquarters.


11 am ......


Ask a policeman ...

Having given you the 'proper Greenwich time', and if
you twist his arm hard enough, he'll admit that all the
pontifical guff about crime detection being ninety-per-cent
perspiration and ten-per-cent inspiration (or whatever the
current popular figures happen to be) is so much hogwash,
and only fit for snouts of hungry pigs. It makes as much
sense as saying 'More people die in hospitals than out of
'em ... therefore, do away with hospitals, and we'll all live
longer.' The perspiration/inspiration gag is based upon
similar cockeyed logic. It sounds neat. It has the sweet ring
of basic truth ... but, this time, the truth is more than a
little cracked.

Crime detection is based upon three things. (1). Going
through the motions; the hoary house-to-house routine,
when circumstances demand: the equally hoary palaver
of 'search', again, when circumstances demand; in short, a
general hithering and thithering in order to create a picture
of high activity ... with the ghost of a hope that some
promising lead might be spewed up in the general mêlée
but, in the main, in order to ensure that the rate-payer feels
that he's getting his money's worth. (2). The sheer, blind
muggery of the criminal classes; the knowledge that most
villains are on the border-line of mental certification; the
certainty that the crook isn't as smart as he thinks he is ...
and, conversely, that the cops aren't as dumb as the crook

thinks *they* are. And (3). Luck ... bloody great dollops of Lady Luck, dropping from heaven and into the laps of eager policemen.

And, of the three requirements, luck is by far the most important.

On this occasion, Lennox caught the luck ... with all the beautiful squelch and spread of an accurately thrown cow-pat!

Lennox, you see, had a very ordinary weakness and, being a man given to mild, personal indulgences, he pandered to this very ordinary weakness. He liked 'elevenses'; he took great, but innocent, enjoyment in the simple act of gulping badly made instant-coffee and chewing arrowroot biscuits. He truly adored arrowroot biscuits, and had done so since a child – indeed, their taste brought back the memory of childhood and, like most grown men, he dreamed of what he *might* have done, had he been granted either foresight or the ability to start life afresh, but with all his present experience of age – therefore, whenever possible, Lennox wandered into the Bordfield H.Q. Typing Pool in time for an invitation from the typists to join them in 'elevenses' ... because *their* instant-coffee was quite abominable, and they *always* had arrowroot biscuits.

He slurped and munched away happily as he wandered between the desks, glancing at the sheets already typed and, sometimes, at the sheets still in the typewriters. He wasn't seeking faults ... he was merely curious.

And the word '*Emmerson*' jumped from the page and hit him.

The sheet was still in the machine, and he bent his bulk slightly forward in order to read what had been typed before, and after, the word 'Emmerson'.

He spoke to the typist.

'This thing, luv.' He nodded at her interrupted work. 'What is it, exactly?'

'A statement, Mr Lennox.'

'Ye-es ... so I see. From a bloke called Lipton. What's it about?'

'That taxi ... yesterday. The one they found burned out.'

'Oh – aye.' Lennox nodded, sagely. 'Who interviewed this Lipton bloke? D'you know?'

'Detective Constable Joyce ... I think.' The typist consulted her scribbling-pad, then said, 'Yes. Detective Constable Joyce.'

'Tell you what, luv.' Lennox placed his cup and saucer on the desk, and picked up the earphones. 'Run the tape back to the beginning ... eh? As a personal favour. To the part where he starts this statement. And lemme hear everything he has to say. Will you do that, please?'

'Of course.'

The typist re-consulted her scribbling-pad, checked a number, held her finger on a button marked 'Reverse' and watched the digits unwind themselves on a dial on the tape-recording machine.

She lifted her finger from the button, and said, 'That's it, Mr Lennox. That's the start of his statement, when you're ready.'

'When you are.' Lennox settled the headset onto his bald pate.

The typist pressed a switch marked 'Start', and a voice spoke into Lennox's ears.

'*... It was yesterday. That would be Monday, the twenty-sixth. At just after eleven. In the morning, that is ...*'

They were on the edge of pothole country – an area of limestone, and the haunt of the so-called 'upside-down mountaineers' – and the youth had never seen a wilder, or more inhospitable, landscape. Like petrified waves in a storm-tossed sea, the crests of the Pennines rolled as far as the eye could see, and in all directions. This place had no identifiable 'valleys'; onto hair-raising dips and great hollows, with knee-deep bracken from which towered jagged cliffs of bare rock.

Garfield braked the truck to a rolling halt, switched off the engine and gazed at the surrounding countryside. There was something not too far removed from love in his eyes.

'Great,' he murmured. 'Majestic. That's the only word I know that really fits ... majestic.'

'It's ...' The youth was about to say something, but changed his mind.

'Come on, Pete.' Garfield smiled. 'Don't be scared. No-body's going to hurt you ... believe me. What was it you wanted to say?'

'It's crazy, Mr Garfield,' said the youth, quietly. 'Up here – this part of wherever we are – it's crazy. And *you're* crazy, Mr Garfield. I'm sorry – maybe I shouldn't have said that ... but you *are*.'

'Yeah ... maybe.' Garfield continued to admire the savage wilderness, around them.

'They'll catch up with you, Mr Garfield.'

'They?'

'The police. They'll catch up with you.'

'Pete,' said Garfield, dreamily, 'nobody catches up with anybody. Nobody even *knows*. Up here, you could use an army ... and still not find another army. It's been done, Pete. Cromwell tried ... and he missed whole villages. Whole monasteries. He knew they were here ... somewhere. He searched for years – for *years*, Pete – and he found some ... but not them all. Dozens – scores – communities who didn't want to be found ... and Cromwell couldn't find them. Use your imagination, Pete. You're a smart boy. Think what that means ... then work out the chances of a few policemen finding us.'

There were a few moments of silence; the silence peculiar to this wild and desolate place – a silence of soft wind-moans and distant curlew-calls ... noises which seemed to add to, rather than break, the silence.

Then, in a slightly unsteady voice, the youth said, 'Can I ask a question, Mr Garfield?'

'Of course, Pete. Anything.'

'And you'll tell me the truth?'

'You have my word, son.'

The youth hesitated, then said, 'This morning – I heard you answering the telephone ... I heard what you said.'

'Oh!' Garfield stared at the distant skyline, and kept his lips rounded after he'd uttered the soft exclamation.

'About the man, Hicks,' said the youth, quietly.

'Hicks?'

'And about daddy.'

'Hicks is dead, Pete.' Garfield turned his head and looked at the youth, as he spoke. 'Shed no tears for Hicks, old son. Hicks was an animal. A brute. Now, he's dead.'

'And daddy?'

'I don't know, Pete ... and that's a fact. I know Hicks was killed in a road accident – in a truck, a lorry, some-thing like that ... and that your father was driving it. I don't know *why* he was driving it. I don't know whether he was hurt – or, if he was hurt, how badly he was hurt ... but I know he isn't dead. I *do* know he's under arrest.'

'Daddy?' The youth looked shocked.

Garfield nodded.

'Why should they arrest daddy? What's *he* done that ...'

'Hicks killed a policeman,' said Garfield, simply.

156

'But you're not saying daddy was with him. You're not saying ...'

'Hicks killed a policeman,' said Garfield. 'We can presume he was on the run. In the truck, or the lorry, or whatever it was. Your father was driving it. *Why* he was driving it ... your guess is as good as mine. But that's why he's under arrest.'

The youth's face crumpled. His lower lip trembled slightly and, for a moment, he almost lost control. Then he fastened his teeth on his lower lip, took a deep breath and spoke in a low, choking voice.

He said, 'I'm only a kid, Mr Garfield ...'

'Pete, did I ever ...'

'... and a coloured kid, at that.'

'Look – I like you, Pete. This isn't a personal thing. I'm not doing this because ...'

'You'd better kill me, Mr Garfield,' gulped the youth.

'Eh?'

'You'd better kill me, Mr Garfield,' said the youth, in a stronger voice. ''Cos, if you don't, I'm going to kill *you*.'

'I'm not going to kill you, Pete.' Garfield sounded shocked at the suggestion. 'For God's sake, son! I'm not even going to *hurt* you.'

The youth stared hatred back at him, and said, 'I mean it, Mr Garfield. First chance I get, I'm going to kill you.'

Noon ......

The waiter jotted the orders onto his pad, as each man consulted the menu and voiced his choice.

Collins said, 'I think, for hors d'oeuvre, I'm going to try your Pâté Maison. Then – for main course – Veal Bergerette.'

'Pâté Maison and Veal Bergerette,' intoned the waiter. 'And vegetables, sir?'

'Creamed potatoes, spinach and – er – baby carrots?'

'Baby carrots, sir,' murmured the waiter.

'That's it, then, thank you.'

'Thank you, sir.' The waiter turned to Crowe, and said, 'And you, sir?'

'Fruit juice,' said Crowe. 'Bitter lemon. Then, deep fried scampi ... with all the trimmings.'

'Yes, sir.' The waiter wrote on his pad, then turned, questioningly towards Lennox.

'What I fancy ain't on the menu, old son,' said Lennox, sadly.

'Sir?'

'Fish and chips ... with bags of vinegar.'

'Er ...' The waiter allowed a slow, twisted smile to touch his lips, then said, 'Might I suggest Haddock Colbert ... with batter?'

Lennox squinted at the menu, then growled, 'Dover Sole Colbert ... that's the only fish dish I see with "Colbert" attached.'

'We have haddock, sir,' the waiter assured him.

'Champion.' Lennox grinned.

'And French Fries?'

'*And* French Fries,' agreed Lennox.

'Peas?' suggested the waiter.

'Mushy?' asked Lennox.

'Fresh, I'm afraid,' said the waiter, apologetically.

Lennox said, 'In that case, no peas. Just fish and chips.'

'And, for hors d'oeuvre, sir?' asked the waiter.

'Grapefruit?' said Lennox, tentatively.

The low smile came again, and the waiter said, 'Without wishing to appear disrespectful, sir ... a glass of Guinness, perhaps?'

'He knows me.' Lennox twisted his head and beamed,

first at Collins, then at Crowe. He grinned up at the waiter, and said, 'You're a man after my own heart, old son. You know a good taste, when you get your mouth round it.'

'Thank you, sir.'

'Guinness it is, son.'

Collins murmured, 'In about thirty minutes, please. Table Number Five ... if that's convenient.'

'I'll see it's reserved, sir.'

'We'll order desserts, when you bring the main course.' His eyes twinkled, as he added, 'Our stout friend will probably want an iced lolly.'

The waiter kept a straight face, and said, 'We can oblige, sir,' and walked away and across the hotel lounge.

'Not nice, Henry,' chided Lennox. 'I'm a man o' simple tastes ... that's all. I may be a slob, but I'm not a childish slob.'

Crowe looked impatient, and said, 'Okay, let's get this briefing under way ... eh?'

The location was the lounge of the *Royale*; classed as Bordfield's premier hotel, it was just that. A.A. and R.A.C. four-star standard, plus an Egon Ronay 'mentioned in despatches'. It had the subdued hum of efficiency of all such hotels; that faint sound of luxury which goes with wall-to-wall pile, a surfeit of well-trained staff and décor which would not disgrace a king's palace. Its sole concession to modernity was in the matter of dress; ties were still a 'must' for dinner, but lounge suits were no longer required before a man was allowed to sit down for lunch. Crowe's outfit was permitted ... albeit with some reluctance. Even Lennox's gear got by with nothing more severe than a tightening of the lips and a quick glance at the ceiling on the part of the immaculately dressed manager.

The three men occupied deep armchairs, in a corner of the lounge and, at Crowe's impatient remark, they hoisted their backsides forward on the padded seats and bent closer into a conspiratorial trio.

'You first, James,' drawled Collins. 'What can your brother-in-law tell us?'

'Okay.' Crowe fished in a pocket of his wind-cheater for cigarettes, as he started. 'About half-twelve ... that's when he got the "or else" message. The greengrocer's shop, across the way ... he was called there, by one of the assistants. A chick named Judy ... he don't know her second name.' He lighted a cigarette, then continued, 'A man's voice. He don't recognise it. No dialect ... nothing like that. Not deep, not high-pitched ... nothing out of the ordinary. Maybe natural ... maybe not. The usual chat. That "they" had Pete ... which means more than one. Thirty big ones to get him back, alive ... and don't tell the cops. Then, the guy rang off.'

'And Hicks?' asked Lennox.

'Hicks rolled up at Christopher Crescent, in the small hours. Nic didn't know about the cop-killing ... how could he? Just that Hicks had Pete. And – Nic didn't know why, didn't *care* why – Hicks wanted out of the district ... that's why.'

'Why the hell ...' began Lennox, then closed his mouth.

'Do I have to spell it out ... *again*?' Crowe favoured Lennox with a wry smile.

'No, old son,' sighed Lennox. 'But it don't make things easier.'

Collins said, 'Your brother-in-law ... does *he* have any ideas?'

'Yeah.' Crowe nodded, slowly. 'Quincey. The big boy who runs the dump where Nic works – *The Blue-Tailed Fly* ... he's been saying things.'

'What things?'

'Double-meanings. Y'know ... hints. Nic thinks Quincey

160

knows a few answers ... maybe. And a coloured chick who works there ... name of Dinah Lemmings. She's been opening her little kisser.'

'They'll have to be seen.'

'By me, skipper,' said Crowe, flatly.

Lennox growled, 'Drag on the handbrake, old son. The way you said that ...'

'I just ask,' said Crowe, blandly. 'Then, they answer.'

'Oh, aye?'

'Two can play it,' murmured Crowe.

'Wassat?'

'The "or else" game.'

Collins said, 'Quincey and Miss Lemmings. It's a start.'

'And,' said Lennox, with the air of a conjurer, producing a herd of elephants from thin air, 'a certain character, name o' Leonard Garfield.'

'I beg your pardon?' said Collins.

'Who's he?' asked Crowe.

Lennox's face shone with the light of self-satisfaction, as he said, 'Right, lads. Tune in your listening equipment ... this isn't guesswork. Leonard Garfield. About twenty past eleven, yesterday morning. He picked up young Emmerson, at Gladstone Comprehensive ... a dud call, saying his dad was in the City Hospital. Taxi, see? From City Taxis. The taxi was a Morris 1100, UGX.9986.T. It was found, burned to a frazzle, just after four, yesterday afternoon. Way and gone to hell, on the moors. Garfield ain't been seen since. Home address, twenty-five Billings Lane ... but his landlady ain't seen him since the snatch.'

'You made a promise, fat man,' said Crowe, tightly. 'No fuzz. This was gonna be ...'

'Here we go again,' sighed Lennox.

'This info didn't come with cornflakes, man. And you ain't had time to ...'

'The bloody taxi,' growled Lennox. He glared at the coloured man, and said, 'I'll not say it again, Sonny Jim. But I don't care a monkey's fart what colour you are. What colour your brother-in-law is. What colour the kid is. You can be polka-dot, for all I care. You can look like a trio of bloody candy-sticks. You get the same treatment. What you *don't* get is preferential treatment.'

'Lenny,' murmured Collins.

'The hell with it,' rumbled Lennox. 'He carries a ruddy great railway sleeper on his shoulder, and everybody has to duck under it. Not *me*, matey. I come up with summat helpful ... and that makes me a liar, does it? Not to you – you know me better – but to this chocolate-coloured goon. And, slob though I may be, I don't go too big a bundle on being ...'

'Cool it, man.' Crowe smiled, shamefacedly. 'You want an apology? You've got it.'

'I want more than an apology,' said Lennox. 'I want an end to all this coloured crap.'

'Okay.' Crowe nodded, solemnly. 'You got that, too.'

'And not just words, wrapped up in hot air.'

'Now, who ain't believing who?' said Crowe.

'Good.' The grin which was never far from Lennox's face returned to its place of residence. He said, 'One more suggestion ... I'll be out-voted, if you both disagree. For what it's worth, I think it's a good idea.'

Collins and Crowe waited.

Lennox said, 'Joyce.'

'Who's she?' asked Crowe.

'She's a he,' explained Lennox. 'Detective Constable Joyce ... the lad who's been following the "disappearing taxi" trick. He knows a few of the answers – not *our* answers ... but answers we could use. He's following Garfield ... as a car thief. The idea I'm putting up for

vote is that we let Joyce keep on following Garfield ...
but, this time, as a kidnapper.'

'You mean letting him in on the closed-shop?' said
Crowe, doubtfully.

'Uhuh.' Lennox nodded.

'Officially?' asked Collins.

'Or unofficially ... we can take a vote on that, too.'

Collins said, 'The obvious question. What's he like?'

'We-ell, he don't *look* like a copper,' said Lennox, slowly.
'That's to his credit. He's very "with it". He ain't frightened
of work ... and he's a mite – er – eccentric.'

'Like you?' suggested Crowe.

'He weighs less,' said Lennox, cheerfully. 'He talks
posher. But – for what it's worth – I think he's a good
lad.'

'*If* he comes in, he comes in unofficially,' said Crowe,
dogmatically.

'If he comes in,' agreed Collins.

Lennox raised his eyebrows and said, 'You're not quite
sure, Henry. That it?'

'It's an odd case. It's a very amateurish case.' Collins
leaned forwards, rested his elbows on the tops of his thighs
and steepled his fingers. It was the posture of the academician, and his tone went with the posture. He said,
'Consider it. First, the money. Thirty-thousand. That's
*not* a large ransom demand ... they talk in half-millions,
and more, these days. Therefore, not professional criminals. Hicks apart, of course ... whom, I think we can
dismiss as merely a necessary appendage to the physical
side of things. Amateurs ... and, moreover, amateurs who
know Emmerson. Garfield? Does this man Garfield know
Emmerson? If so, has Emmerson mentioned his football
pool win to Garfield? Or, has the son mentioned it to
Garfield? If not, to whom *have* either of them mentioned it,

who might, in turn, have mentioned it to Garfield?

'But, always – and we must never lose sight of this – *amateurs*. Don't treat them as professionals ... whoever they are, and however many there are. Don't credit them with *planning*. They haven't had *time* to plan. Little more than a week ago, this thing would have been impossible ... Emmerson wouldn't have had the money to meet their demands. Therefore, this was a spur-of-the-moment kidnapping. No carefully arranged hiding place. No detailed arrangement for receiving the money. A completely off-the-cuff thing. Not by Hicks ... I think we can safely rule out Hicks. Possibly by this man Garfield. Possibly by some person we don't yet know about. But, it's a flimsy structure, gentlemen. It shouldn't take too much breaking.'

'In a nutshell, skipper,' said Crowe, softly. 'But, inside that husk's a kid I ain't gonna see hurt.'

Lennox rubbed his bald head, meditatively, and said, 'Tell you what. Jim ... you take up home at Christopher Crescent. At your brother-in-law's place. I'll fix things so any friends can visit him for a chin-wag. You brief him to let 'em all know you're staying there.'

Crowe murmured, 'Nice,' as understanding dawned.

'They can't get at Emmerson,' rumbled Lennox. 'And, if they could, *he* couldn't get at the cash. They might try *you* as a backdoor way of reaching him.'

'It's worth a try,' agreed Collins.

'And this cat Joyce?' asked Crowe.

Lennox said, 'I'm in favour.'

'I'm inclined to agree,' said Collins.

'But – y'know ... off the record. Eh?' said Crowe.

Lennox said, 'It might be better. Leave that side o' things with me.'

'Tell him,' said Crowe. '*The Blue-Tailed Fly*. Tonight

164

'... say, ten-thirty. I'll be there, if he's interested.'

They talked a little longer, and the talk cemented a friendship, between Crowe and Lennox which, by this time, was
already firm. They dotted the i's and crossed the t's of an
under-the-counter campaign against Garfield, and against
whoever else had assisted in the design to hold the youth
to ransom. It was a very flexible campaign ... it *had* to be,
in view of the fact that they didn't yet know the strength,
or cunning of their enemy.

It was, in one respect, a strange conversation. It was
strange, in that, while all three men spoke the truth, none
of them spoke the *whole* truth. And yet, none of them
consciously lied.

Collins ...

The truth was that, deep inside his scholarly brain, a
tiny grain of intelligence stirred at the thought of one last
chase; at the realisation that, for a few precious hours –
for a few days, at the most – he could revert to the role
he had played and enjoyed for more than half a lifetime.

The man-hunter. The chess-master, whose board was a
whole police district, and whose pieces were living people.

Lennox ...

Inside his fat hide, his heart beat that much more happily
at the thought of playing a one-off game, against hidebound
authority; his was the eccentric's joy of cocking a snook at
an establishment, of which he was a square-peg–round-hole
part, and justifying his eccentricity.

Crowe ...

With Crowe, it was skin pigmentation. Colour against
colour ... although he would have denied it, and believed
in his denial. His nephew – a coloured youth – had been
kidnapped and (without much doubt) white men had kidnapped him. Those white men had to be found and, when

165

found, *all* white men had to be shown that coloured kids were sacrosanct. And, to that end, he was prepared to use other white men ... Collins, Lennox and, if necessary, this unknown cat, Joyce.

Lies. Lies which were not lies, in that they were unconscious lies. They nudged the conversation; they turned mere words into masks, behind which hid the truth.

It was just a conversation ... like most other conversations.

And the man called 'Al'.

Nobody talked to 'Al' unless he invited talk. He was a cold man, without emotion. He smiled rarely, and laughed not at all. Life, and the vicissitudes of his own life, had tempered him; robbed him of all feeling; built around him a near-impregnable shell. He was not liked, by his fellow-men. Nor was he disliked ... because, even dislike requires some degree of involvement, and the man called 'Al' refused his fellow-men even *that* degree of involvement.

And yet ...

Within his shell, he wept silently, at memories and at might-have-beens.

A wife who understood, perhaps? A partner, who realised the torment of the introvert with a passion for an outgoing calling? That one word – 'passion' ... why had she never understood its meaning? To be a good cook – to be house-proud – to be the perfect hostess – to dress smartly and talk intelligently – to be almost beautiful, and to retain that near-beauty into her middle-years ... but, to be without passion.

Her passion, had she been capable of passion, might have changed him. It might have given him confidence enough to laugh. Confidence enough to meet his fellow-men as equals and, therefore, as friends.

So many times ... the thought of that adage, which contained a centre of truth.

'Behind every successful man, there is a woman.'

Ah! ... but, behind every failure, there is *also* a woman.

The man called 'Al' chewed his way through a lonely meal. Lonely, as all his meals were lonely – as every meal he had ever eaten had been lonely ... as his whole *life* had been lonely.

Albert Denning, senior maths master at Gladstone Comprehensive School, lowered the fork, with which he had been eating sliced melon, leaned forward and sideways, in order to talk across the front of the deputy head, and said, 'Headmaster ... might I ask what is happening to the boy Emmerson?'

'I beg your pardon?'

'If you care to change places, Mr Denning,' said the deputy head, irritably.

'No – not at all, sir – I merely wished to ask the headmaster ...'

Adams looked cross, and said, 'Can't it wait, Mr Denning?'

'It – er – it seems important, sir. A personal opinion, of course, but ...'

'I don't *mind* changing places.'

'No ... I wouldn't dream of it, deputy.'

'Mr Denning,' said Adams, coldly, 'there is an unwritten rule, as far as this dining-room is concerned.'

'Yes, sir. I know, but ...'

'We do *not* talk shop.'

'Quite, headmaster. But, it isn't ...'

'Shop, religion and politics ... the three forbidden subjects, Mr Denning. Need I remind you?'

'No, headmaster. Nevertheless ...'

'You have a free period, this afternoon?'

'Yes, sir. From three o'clock, until ...'

'Shall we say my office, at three-fifteen?'

'It's – it's not that ...'

'Why on earth are you concerning yourself about the boy, Denning?' snapped the deputy head. 'He's one of Finchley's little horrors, isn't he?'

'Yes, deputy, but ...'

In a bad-tempered tone, the deputy head said, 'We run a school here, Denning. Not a family advice unit. We do our best to instil some degree of discipline into potential hooligans ... plus, God help us, certain basic learning. We fail, Denning. We invariably fail. Therefore, why not forget our failure, whenever possible?'

'We don't *always* fail, deputy,' said Adams, and it was a mild reprimand. 'Occasionally we succeed.' He turned to his left, and continued, 'Wouldn't you agree, Finchley?'

'Yes, sir. I'd most certainly agree.'

Finchley was a morose man, who kept himself to himself and rarely spoke unless spoken to first.

Denning leaned even farther across the table and spoke to Finchley, across both the deputy and the headmaster.

He said, 'Alfred ... you should know. What *is* going to happen to young Emmerson? He's your pupil, so you should ...'

'The weather,' interrupted Adams, in a very pointed and very penetrating tone, 'is uncommonly mild for late October. I think we might be in for a very unseasonable winter. Don't you, gentlemen?'

The cave was a shallow grotto, under a limestone overhang. One of nature's bolt-holes, wherein prehistoric man might once have sheltered from the oncoming ice, or the prowling sabre-tooth.

168

The lorry was in a ravine, about two miles away; smashed and bracken-covered and beyond all hope of recovery without chains and winches.

The youth's wrists were still tied behind his back, with nylon baler-twine. He sat on a boulder and gulped air, to regain his breath after the slog up the slope to the cave.

3 pm . . . . . .

Emmerson hadn't quite come up with a clear focus on the full picture.

A couple of times he'd eased a hand from under the sheets and touched the bandage around his skull and – okay, that was okay – he remembered the dog, and the concrete lamp-standard coming up at a terrifying speed.

And – okay, that, too, was okay – the strange men who'd asked all the questions (and the strange man who still sat in the chair, alongside the bed) were all policemen.

But, after that . . .

'I ain't a bad man, God. You know that. I don't have to tell *you* that. I ain't too clever. I've done some pretty stupid things in this life . . . and some things I ain't too proud of, at that. But I ain't bad. Not *bad*! I mean . . . what the hell (sorry, God) – but what's the reason for all these policemen? I ain't told 'em about Pete, have I? While I was unconscious . . . you didn't let me tell 'em about Pete. You wouldn't do a thing like that to me, would you? No-o . . . I know you wouldn't do *that*, God. So, why all these policemen taking all this interest? Why *me*? I had an accident . . . but accidents happen all the time. Yeah – I know – Jim told me . . . something. I don't rightly remember what.

169

Something about a man called Hicks. Something about murder ... the murder of a policeman. Who's Hicks, God? I don't know anybody called Hicks. And, sure as hell (sorry, God) – but I ain't mixed up in the murder of any policeman. I got grief enough, God. You know that ... you know I ain't gonna mix myself up in the murder of a policeman. So, what's happening, God? I ain't *that* bad. Surely you can let me know what's happening ... ?'

Lipton was a very busy man. A man with more work than he could cope with. Had you asked him, he would have told you that running a large taxi firm was no penny-ante affair; that the boss-man had to be on the ball, every minute of every day ... otherwise, the twisting hounds who sat behind the steering wheels, would have all the cream from the top of the milk, and City Taxis would be just about as useful as a gumboil.

Lipton snarled, 'Judas priest! I've already taken time off to tell the tale to some pansy-boy detective. I've done a Bing Crosby act into a microphone, at the bloody nick. And, if you think I'm ...'

'Cool it, man,' snapped Crowe.

'You can go straight to hell, for all I ...'

'I need to know about Garfield.'

'Sod Garfield. When I get my hands on Garfield, I'll ...'

'After you, with Garfield.'

'Get out of here!' bawled Lipton. 'Get the hell out of this ...'

Crowe said, 'No way, man,' and, at the same time, grabbed Lipton by the tie, jerked him out of his chair and slammed him, hard, against a steel filing-cabinet which was handily placed against one wall of the office. Crowe repeated, 'No way, man,' in a soft drawl as he used his free hand to belt a fist into Lipton's gut.

Beyond the picture window, the man with the scarred face and eye-patch frowned and made as if to stand up. Crowe shook his head, warningly, and the man with the scarred face and the eye-patch decided to mind his own business, and concentrated all his attention upon his clipboard.

Crowe transferred his grip, from the tie to the lapels of Lipton's jacket, dumped Lipton back into his chair, and said, 'Garfield, friend. Tell me about Garfield.'

'You – you – you ...' Lipton held his middle and struggled for air. He gasped, 'What – what the hell. You can't *do* this.'

'I already have,' Crowe reminded him.

'I'll – I'll ...'

'You'll tell me about Garfield, friend.'

'Sod Garfield. *Bugger* Garfield. I don't ever want to see ...'

'I don't know him. Just his name.'

'You're missing damn-all.'

'Okay ... tell me what I'm missing.'

'Why the hell should I? Who the hell *are* you ... ?'

The sentence ended in a yelp of frightened pain, as Crowe grabbed a handful of hair with one hand, and slapped Lipton across the mouth with the other.

'*I*,' said Crowe, calmly, 'am the guy who is asking questions about Garfield ... and *you* are the guy who's gonna answer 'em.'

'Okay – okay ... no more rough stuff. Okay?' Lipton raised open hands to shoulder height, in surrender. 'I – I – I'm not a violent man.'

'Yeah ... me, too,' said Crowe.

'Christ!'

'So, tell me about Garfield, and we both stay happy.'

'He's a – he's a ...' Lipton waved his hands, vaguely.

'Yeah?' encouraged Crowe.

'An over-educated twat,' exploded Lipton.

'Specifically?'

'Y'know ... university. Sociology ... I think.'

'And?'

'Y'know what they're like.'

'I want to know what Garfield's like.'

'Like the rest of 'em.' Crowe drew back his clenched fist, and Lipton hurriedly continued, 'You see 'em on every protest march. The berk with the banner. The nut case with all the bright ideas, but no brains.'

'Socialist?'

'Uhuh.' Lipton shook his head. '*I'm* a Socialist ... and a million miles from those kinky bleeders.'

'Communist?' suggested Crowe.

'Could be ... I never asked.'

'You don't sound too sure.'

'You want the truth?' said Lipton, almost confidentially.

In a very deadpan voice, Crowe said, 'Unless you want a going over.'

'Oh! Er – well ... the truth is, I don't think the stupid fink *knows* what he is. Y'know – free beef for all, but don't kill no cows ... that sorta crap. Everybody's his friend – he thinks ... he hopes. There ain't no shit in the world, so nothing stinks. He sees a tree full of apples, and he figures they're all his. They're there for the taking – the fruits of nature, and all that crap ... and screw the poor sod who's worked his guts out, growing 'em. Y'know the sort. Do-gooders. Parasites. Sure – they're willing to give the world everything they own ... which is pretty easy, because they don't own a damn thing. That's Garfield, mac. A pain in the arse ... and, whenever he's short, he rolls in here, and I'm mug enough to give him work until he's earned a few more quid.'

172

'Honest?' asked Crowe.

'Eh?'

'Is he honest? Does he fleece you?'

'Sure he's honest.' Lipton looked indignant. 'Would I trust him with a car ... ?' He stopped, frowned, then corrected himself. '*Was* honest. Till yesterday. After yesterday, I wouldn't trust him with a paper-clip.'

'You mean the taxi?'

'What else? He takes a good Morris, drives it to who-knows-where, then fires it, for who-knows-why. After that ... *nothing*!'

'There's a man called Hicks ...' began Crowe.

'Hold it, mac.' Lipton raised a hand, palm outwards. 'Hicks I know about ... I heard it on the news. I read it, in the Stop Press. Hicks, as I read it, killed a cop. The fuzz have been round, already. They quizzed my boy, in the next room. Hicks, I want nothing to do with.'

'Hicks is dead,' said Crowe.

'Yeah ... they tell me.'

'So, unless you do grave-digging as a hobby, there isn't much you *can* do with Hicks. Right?'

'You know what I mean, mac.'

'I want the connection,' insisted Crowe.

'He worked here ... that's all. Just a little. A long time ...'

'Between Hicks and Garfield,' interrupted Crowe.

'They both worked here. Both part-time. That's all.'

Crowe said, 'Okay – other than that, what had they in common?'

'Eh?' Lipton's eyes widened.

'Garfield. Hicks. Where were they alike?'

'Jesus wept! Two arms – two legs ... beyond that, nothing.'

'Beliefs? Principles? Politics?'

'Hey, mac.' There was near-disbelief in Lipton's tone. 'Hicks? He believed in muscle ... that's all. Principles? ... he wouldn't have known how to pronounce the word. And *politics*? ... not since Mosley sacked his bully-boys. Hicks – Jesus Christ! ... I doubt if he knew how to draw a cross on a voting paper.'

'Okay,' said Crowe, patiently, 'let's get back to Garfield.'

'Look – I've told you all I ...'

'Married?'

'You kidding?'

'No ... I'm asking.'

'Dames are dumb ... but never *that* dumb.'

'Parents?'

'I guess ... unless he was hatched. He never mentioned.'

'Where was he born?'

'Christ knows.'

'When he wasn't working here, what?'

'He drew Social Security. I keep telling you ...'

'It's not a bottomless well, friend.'

'The Garfields all think so.'

'Not easy. Not so easy, for single men.'

'Okay.' Lipton's mouth moved into a half-sneer. 'He picks a little corn up at some youth club thing.'

'Where?'

'Look, mac – I've answered enough ...'

'*Where?*'

Lipton jerked, as the repeated question hit him, like a bullet.

'Hey, man,' warned Crowe, icily. 'I say when. When I've asked all the questions, and when you've supplied all the answers ... that's when. Now, you get this thing straight, friend. I'm gonna get answers. You are going to provide them, free of charge ... or I am gonna slap 'em outa you. And, I don't give one tiny damn which. And *that* – Lipton, old buddy, old buddy – is exactly when. You get it?'

Lipton looked shocked, and breathed, 'And you complain, when people call you savages.'

Crowe showed his teeth, in a quick, tiger-smile, and said, 'You keep believing that, man ... and keep the answers coming.'

'The Bordfield Youth Centre,' said Lipton, heavily.

'And?'

'It's a dump. Good intentions ... like all these things. A ping-pong outfit and a record player ... assuming they haven't been smashed to hell by this time.'

'Where?'

'A prefab, do-it-yourself hut. Tenby Street.'

'Where's Tenby Street?'

'Off Christopher Crescent. That's ...'

'I know where Christopher Crescent is. And Garfield runs this Youth Centre.'

'Helps. He hangs around – y'know ... organising the disorder. The man who runs it is Lambert. Alexis Lambert. For my money, he's a raving queer.'

'Uhuh.' Crowe nodded, slowly, then said, 'And *The Blue-Tailed Fly*?'

'It's – er – it's a night club.' Lipton looked puzzled.

'Yeah – I know – but where does Garfield fit in?'

'Where?'

'*The Blue-Tailed Fly?*'

'You must be joking.'

'This isn't a comic act, Lipton. You need proof? Okay – just get smart a little, and ...'

'You *must* be joking,' protested Lipton. 'Garfield? Jesus! ... he couldn't afford to drink *water* there, at the prices *they* charge.'

'As a backroom employee, then?'

'I wouldn't know ... but I doubt it.'

'Why?'

'Principles ... the usual crappy garbage. It ain't yours, so you want no part. You know the patter. And – y'know ... these creeps really think they mean it. They mouth their ...'

'Hicks?' snapped Crowe.

'What about Hicks?'

'How does he link in with *The Blue-Tailed Fly*?'

'No way, mac ... not that I know of.' Lipton shook his head. 'Hicks was pure granite, from the eyes north. Quincey – that's the guy who runs ...'

'Yeah, I've heard of Quincey.'

'He uses muscle – they all do ... but Quincey's muscle has brains attached. He'd never use a stone-age gink like Hicks.'

'Sure?'

Lipton put outrage into his expression, and said, 'You want lies? ... okay, I'll make you happy and give you lies. Quincey used Hicks. But the truth is he didn't. He *wouldn't*. I know him too well. Now, take your pick, mac. Whichever answer makes you happy.'

'Don't get smart-arsed, Lipton,' said Crowe, softly.

'Me?' The outrage was suddenly very genuine. '*Me?* Mac, I would remind you. This is my office. My firm. My whole outfit. And you come here, smacking *me* around – asking *me* a million and one stupid questions – shoving your sticky fingers up *my* tender nostrils ... and now you have the gall to tell *me* not to get smart-arsed! I dunno who the hell you are, mac, but I want you out of here ... *now.*'

'Sure.' Crowe grinned, and eased himself towards the door.

'And – just for a favour – don't come back ... eh?'

'Who knows, man?' Crowe chuckled as he opened the

**176**

door, to leave the office. 'Y'know – who knows? ... savages
are pretty unpredictable.'

The youth said, 'Mr Garfield, I want to pee.'

Garfield turned from the mouth of the cave and eyed
the youth with worried suspicion.

'I do,' insisted the youth.

Garfield sucked his upper lip, and tried to reach a decision.

'I can't hold it much longer, Mr Garfield,' said the
youth.

Garfield nodded, walked into the cave, and said, 'All right,
Pete. Turn around.'

The youth turned. Garfield untied the nylon twine; it
took him some time to loosen the knots. Throughout, the
youth stood perfectly still, and made no move to either run
away or attack his captor.

Garfield said, 'Okay, Pete. At the back of the cave.'

While the youth urinated, Garfield stooped and picked
up a flat piece of limestone; a piece big enough to hold in
the fist, and use as a weapon.

The stone wasn't needed.

Having relieved himself the youth walked meekly back
to where Garfield was waiting, turned and held his wrists
behind his back, ready to receive the twine.

Garfield re-lashed the wrists together, and the youth made
no protest ... he was too busy concentrating on bulging his
muscles as much as possible, in order to create a certain
amount of slack in the twine; when it was fastened he
relaxed the tension.

Lennox glared up, from behind his posh desk, in his posh
office, and snarled, 'You have informants, lad. I want their
names.'

177

'I'm sorry, sir.'

Joyce stood rigidly to attention, and stared at a spot on the wall, directly above, and behind, Lennox's bald skull.

'There's a reason,' said Lennox, harshly.

'Yes, sir.'

'It's not just idle curiosity.'

'No, sir.'

'The reason's none of your business ... but it's important.'

'Yes, sir.'

'So, we'll have 'em, shall we? The name of every informant you've ever used.'

Joyce swallowed, then croaked, 'I'm sorry, sir.'

'Sorry?' Lennox pushed his podgy chin forward, aggressively. 'Just what the hell does that mean, lad? That you haven't any informants?'

'No, sir.' Joyce moistened his lips, and continued to stare, fixedly at the spot on the wall. He said, 'I have informants, sir. Every detective officer has informants.'

'Bent bastards,' sneered Lennox.

Joyce hesitated, then said, 'Some are no better than they should be, sir. But I don't do any horse-trading. When they step out of line, they get clobbered. They're in no doubt ... before I even *ask* for information.'

'That's what *you* say.'

'Sir – with respect – I object to being called a liar.'

'Do you? By Christ, *do* you?' Lennox allowed alien contempt to make the questions ugly. Then, he snapped, '*Without* respect, lad – because I happen to be a few rungs up the ladder from you – I object to a categorical refusal to obey my orders. And that's what it is, Joyce – an order ... you'll tell me the names of your informants. Now!'

'No, sir,' said Joyce in a tight voice.

'I'm not going to publish 'em. They'll go no farther

178

than this office ... if that's what's worrying you.'

'No, sir,' repeated Joyce, doggedly.

'For Christ's sake, *why?*' exploded Lennox.

Joyce held himself ramrod stiff, and spoke from behind tight-closed teeth.

He said, 'Sir, your request – your order – is not in line with police practice. Standard practice. Sources of information carry the implied warranty of absolute confidentiality. Were it otherwise, no informant would ever trust his detective officer ... and a lot of crime would remain undetected.'

Joyce stopped, and Lennox said, 'Go on. I'm interested.'

Joyce continued, 'That's it, sir. I don't *like* informants – I don't know many officers who do – but I use them ... and I make sure they don't use me. If I divulged their names – even to you – and if they ever found out, the results could be very serious. Word would get around, and every other informant – men who give *real* information, to better detectives than myself – might not feel safe any more. They'd clam up. The crime detection rate would suffer.' Joyce paused, then added, 'If one of them's on the twist – and it's possible – I suggest the matter be handed to some other detective officer, for investigation. I'll not hinder him. I'll not shield a criminal ... even if he's one of my informants. But I can't name names, sir. It's a matter of principle.'

'Is it, now?' mused Lennox. 'And, exactly how far are you prepared to go, on this matter of principle?'

'Back to the beat, sir,' said Joyce, hoarsely.

'As far as that?'

Joyce almost whispered, 'My resignation ... if that becomes necessary, sir.'

Lennox chuckled. Joyce lowered his eyes for a split second, saw the pudding face wobbling around, atop the multiple chins, came to the quick conclusion that the Head of the C.I.D. had, at last, lost what few marbles he had left in his bag, and returned his gaze to the wall.

'Sit down, lad,' wheezed Lennox.

'Sir, if you don't mind, I'd rather ...'

'Sit down,' repeated Lennox. 'It was a come-on. I had to be sure.'

'Sure, sir?'

'There's summat I want you to do, old son. Summat you can refuse – and no hard feelings ... but, either way, summat you'll have to keep tucked tightly under your bonnet. See?'

Joyce relaxed a little, looked nonplussed, then said, 'Sir ... this could still be a come-on.'

'It could be, but it ain't,' grinned Lennox. 'Don't worry, son. Nobody's going to ask you for names. This has to do with something that's – er – y'know ... very much off the record. *Very* much off the record. And *my* hide's at stake. So-o, don't blame me for being canny, old son. I need to know how far folks can be trusted to keep their mouths shut. You, for example.'

Joyce relaxed a little more, and nodded.

'Sorry,' apologised Lennox.

'Sir?'

'For performing the top-blowing routine.'

'Oh! That's – er – that's quite all right, sir.'

'Now ... unfasten your corsets, sit down and listen.'

Joyce returned a smile for the grin, sat down and listened.


4 pm ......


Garfield stood at the mouth of the cave, stared at the sky and the oncoming October gloom and, deep inside himself,

180

knew that this thing was going to turn sour ... as always.

As everything he touched turned sour. As every decent belief, and every action group he'd ever supported, had *always* turned sour.

Christ!

The number of lost causes he'd supported. The number of times he'd tried to nudge civilisation just that one notch forward. Anti-blood-sports. Squatting rights; the abomination of thousands of empty houses, and thousands of homeless families. Factory farming; the inhumanity of money-grabbing brutes, when it came to a matter of the lesser creatures who also shared this world. Pollution; air pollution, river pollution, sea pollution, food pollution ... the pollution of the whole bloody planet, by blind idiots, who couldn't recognise self-destruction, even when it was spelled out for them.

And violence ...

It was all violence. Everything ... it all boiled down to some form of violence. The violence of man against man. The violence of man against nature. International violence. Industrial violence. Marital violence. God! ... so many faces – so many permutations – of the same rotten disease.

*Violence.*

He turned, slowly, stared at the youth in silence for a few moments, then said, 'Don't think it's all like this, Pete.'

'What?' asked the youth.

'The world. It's not *all* rotten.'

'You mean, like you, Mr Garfield?'

'Me?' Garfield looked shocked at the suggestion.

'What you're doing,' said the youth.

'Nobody's going to hurt you, Pete,' said Garfield, sadly.

'You keep saying that.'

'It's true. Not while I'm around.'

'But you already *have*.'

'No – you can't say that ... not me. Hicks, perhaps. He hit you with ...'

'You're part of it, Mr Garfield,' insisted the youth. 'Look at daddy. He's hurt. I'm here ... tied up, like this. You're part of it.'

'The means ... that's all,' explained Garfield. 'The end. Certain means are justified.'

'You're a wicked man, Mr Garfield,' said the youth, gently. 'You pretend not to be ... but you *are*.'

'No.' Garfield shook his head, slowly. 'On the surface, maybe. But it's the world, Pete. The world stinks. The world's wicked ... not me. I wouldn't hurt anybody. I don't *want* to hurt anybody. But the world doesn't leave much choice ... so I want out. I want to find somewhere. Y'know ... peaceful. Away from the rat-race. I need money. That's all.'

'Take me home,' said the youth, simply. 'I'll talk to daddy. He'll give you the fare, to wherever it is you want to go ... I know he will. He's a good man. He'll understand.'

'I wish I could, Pete.' The twisted, non-humorous smile lent truth to the remark. 'Y'know that, Pete ... I *really* wish I could.'

'What's to stop you?' asked the youth.

'It's – er ...' Garfield thrust his hands into his trouser pockets, half-turned from the youth, and said, 'These things. They're not single-handed. Otherwise ...'

He left the sentence unfinished.

'Hicks?' said the youth.

'Hicks is dead,' muttered Garfield.

'The man you call Al?'

'You shouldn't listen, Pete,' sighed Garfield. 'Just me – see? ... if you'll take good advice. Hicks, if you like ... but Hicks is dead. So-o, just me. When you get back, they'll ask questions. Tell them what they want to know ... Len

182

Garfield. That's all. They'll be satisfied. Leave it at that.'

'But it's *not* just you. It's not even just you and Hicks.'

'Pete!' The name was almost a groan. 'Leave it. Be advised ... *leave it*.'

The place had a smell of its own; a mix of damp, stale cigarette smoke and accumulated dust. There was a raised dais, at one end; a tiny stage, without drapes and without backdrop. There was a battered and scratched piano in front of, and to one side of, the dais. A table-tennis table stood in the middle of the bare-boarded floor; a table-tennis table which had suffered rough usage, and whose surface was bowed and almost broken. Torn posters broke the monotony of the colour-wash walls; posters held in position by strips of yellowing Sellotape at each corner. There was a huge cupboard in one corner of the room; a monstrosity from some ancient office, and which might not have looked out of place surrounded by stand-up desks but which, in any other surroundings, *had* to look ugly. There were three light bulbs, equidistant from each other along the centre of the ceiling, and each hanging from frayed flex, and unshaded.

Bordfield Youth Centre.

Lipton had described it as a dump, and Crowe was prepared to second Lipton's opinion. Lipton had also voiced an opinion about Alexis Lambert – the man in charge of Bordfield Youth Centre ... and Crowe was prepared to go along with *that* opinion, too.

Lambert was a 'toucher'; whenever the opportunity presented itself – and often when physical contact was quite unnecessary – Lambert allowed his fingers to stroke, caress, prod and poke. The arm, the wrist, the elbow, the back – anywhere ... just as long as there was gentle contact.

Crowe held himself in check. His every instinct was to slap this slimy creep in the mouth ... but that wouldn't have helped. The object of the exercise was to get information. As much information as possible. And, with this she-man, fist work would merely have brought on screaming hysteria.

'Oh, yes, I know him.' Lambert spoke in a voice which was a few semitones too high, and with the hint of a lisp. 'He's a great friend of mine.'

'He helps here ... so I'm told.'

'Yes. He's a great help. I don't know how I'd manage without him.'

'He's missing,' said Crowe.

'Really?' Lambert raised his eyebrows and cocked his head, interestedly.

'Since yesterday morning.'

'Really?' Lambert repeated the eyebrows and head trick.

Almost off-handedly, Crowe said, 'Er – Chief Superintendent Collins thought *you* might be able to help.'

It wasn't the strict truth. It should have been *ex*-Chief Superintendent Collins ... and visiting the Bordfield Youth Centre had been Crowe's idea. Therefore, it wasn't the strict truth – but, on the other hand, it wasn't *quite* a full-blooded lie ... and it had the required effect.

Lambert squealed, 'Oh!' and backed off a pace. Then he smiled his most fetching smile, and said, 'I didn't know we had any darkies in the police force, in these parts.'

'We get everywhere,' said Crowe, mildly. 'A few more boatloads, and we'll take over.'

'Oh, *you*!' yelped Lambert, rocked forward far enough to push Crowe playfully on the shoulder, then collapsed into peals of high-pitched giggling laughter.

'Garfield,' Crowe reminded him, in a business-like voice.

'Oh, yes ... Len.'

'Where is he?'

'I haven't the foggiest, dear boy. He's a little strange, you know.'

'Strange?'

'Odd.'

'In what way, odd?'

'Funny ideas. Y'know ... *funny*. Funny ideas.'

'Hilarious? Peculiar? Or just plain barmy?'

'Barmy. I'd call them *barmy*. I've told him. I've said ...'

'Specifically?' said Crowe. 'Tell me where he *might* be. Where you wouldn't be surprised if he *is*.'

'We-ell, now ...' Lambert rested a forefinger on his lower lip. 'Women ... he goes with women, sometimes. He could be *there*.'

'Which women?'

'Oh, just women. Any old women – we-ell, not *old* women ... but y'know what I mean. Just any woman he can pick up.'

'Any particular girl friend?'

'No. He hasn't mentioned ... and he *would*. Knowing Len, he *would*. We're very close, you see.'

'If not women, what?' asked Crowe.

'Anywhere. Anywhere at all, dear boy. You can never tell with Len.'

'Where might he hide?' asked Crowe, bluntly.

'Hide? Why? Why should he ... ?'

'Answer – don't ask ... where *might* he hide?'

'Oh, a thousand places. *Thousands*.'

'Name a few.'

'We-ell, I ... Really – I don't know ... anywhere, I suppose.'

'You're close, you say.'

'Oh, yes. Very close.'

'So, come on, man. *Where?*'

Lambert pressed his forefinger into his lower lip, plastered a concentrative expression across his face, and pondered.

Then, he mused, 'Y'see, he's so many *friends*, dear boy. So many! He's very *popular*. Everybody ... everybody likes Len. The boys who come here, for example. They all *love* him. I don't think – no-o ... I can't think of a single person who doesn't like Len. First-name terms. Always. Within minutes, it's first-name terms. And always shortened. With me, for instance ... it's always Al. Never Alex. Never Alexis. I don't particularly like Al – it sounds so *gangsterish*, if you see what I mean ... but it's Len's way. Friendly – with everybody ... shortened first name, in next to no time. We have a boy comes here – such a nice boy – Edward ... and Len *always* calls him Ed. Nobody else. Just Len. And I don't think Edward likes it, but ...'

And, so it went on. The prattle. The fairy-floss waffle which Lambert mistook for conversation. It went on for more than forty-five minutes. Pointed questions, blunted by simpering, long-winded answers.

Crowe marvelled ... that so many words could add up to so little.

But Crowe wasn't a cop.

Any experienced cop could have told him. That's the way it goes, and the trick is to pick up the feel of the pearl, hidden in the six-inch-thick eiderdown.

Meanwhile, at Lessford ...

The Mini-Cooper looked unbecoming in the sombre, Victorian cul-de-sac; like a splash of psychedelic dazzle, daubed on a Landseer painting.

Inside the flat, Joyce was meeting a man he'd heard about; a man around whose name legends were already being woven. A slim man, with the air of an academician; quietly, but immaculately, dressed; a man who, but for his natural manner and charm, might have been mistakenly thought to be a poseur. The word 'gentleman' snagged on the hooks of Joyce's mind ... the true meaning of that word, as it might be used by (say) Miss Benson.

And that, too, was odd ... that almost every thought which now entered Joyce's mind was measured against a yardstick used by Agatha Benson.

Joyce sat in one of the wing-chairs, while Collins scrutinised the file of documents which Joyce had brought from Bordfield Headquarters.

Collins leaned forward, and placed the file on the settle.

He smiled at Joyce, and said, 'Do you drink?'

'Yes, sir.' Then, Joyce saw fit to add the qualification of 'A little'.

'Sherry? Whisky? Brandy? That's the only choice I can offer, I'm afraid.'

'Sherry, please.'

'Please make yourself comfortable, Mr Joyce.'

'Er – yes, sir. Thank you, sir.'

Having placed the drinks on the military-chest table, Collins resumed his position in the other wing-chair.

They sipped their drinks.

Collins said, 'This man, Garfield – the driver of the taxi ... he's obviously one of the kidnappers.'

'Obviously, sir.'

'And Hicks, of course.'

'Chief Superintendent Lennox explained the possible connection, before I left.'

'More than "possible",' murmured Collins. 'Fairly certain, I think.'

'Yes, sir. So do I ... now it's been explained to me.'

Collins said, 'The taxi was burned.'

'Yes, sir.'

'Presumably to destroy clues. Fingerprints, and the like.'

'It seems so.'

'Out on the moors, somewhere.'

'Miles from anywhere.'

'So-o ...' Collins sipped at the sherry. 'Somebody knows his way through that wilderness. Knows the roads and the cart-tracks. Knows where you can take a motor car, set fire to it, in secret, and be able to get clear without anybody seeing you.'

'That's about the size of it.'

'Not Hicks, of course.' Collins stared at the sherry in his glass as he spoke. He seemed to be voicing his thoughts, rather than expressing an opinion. 'Hicks was, primarily, an urban animal. He probably knew his way *across* the moors, but that's about as far as his knowledge of the moors would have gone. The chances are very much against him knowing the secret places.'

'He – er – he could have been a passenger, sir,' suggested Joyce.

'Three people?' Collins eyed the sherry, quizzically. 'Garfield, the Emmerson youth and Hicks? Then, three people having to make a run for it? Dangerous? ... wouldn't you say? Assuming the plan called for the destruction of the taxi, immediately after the kidnapping ... I think we can assume that. It follows that, however hurriedly it was arranged, a bolt-hole was waiting ... therefore, why not the bolt-hole first, *then* the destruction of the taxi?'

'You mean Hicks stayed with the boy, while Garfield drove the ...'

'I favour the other way round, Mr Joyce,' drawled Collins. '*Garfield* staying at the bolt-hole, with the boy, while Hicks took the taxi and destroyed it.'

'But – sir – you've already said that Hicks wouldn't know the side-roads across ...'

188

'He could have been told. He might even have been taken there. Shown.'

'Yes, sir. But ...'

'Hicks was on the loose, last night, Mr Joyce,' said Collins, gently. 'Now – assuming *Garfield* drove the taxi to its place of destruction – that would mean he returned to the bolt-hole, relieved Hicks ... who, in turn, went to Bordfield. Unnecessary comings and goings, don't you think? Whereas, if they *all* went to the bolt-hole, then *Hicks* took the taxi, and destroyed it, prior to visiting Bordfield, getting drunk, being involved in a brawl – and all the rest of it ... A more simple reconstruction, wouldn't you agree?'

'Yes, sir,' sighed Joyce.

'More sherry?' asked Collins.

'No, sir. No, thank you.' Joyce hesitated, then said, 'Well, sir ... what do you suggest?'

'The answer ...' Collins leaned forward, picked the file from the settle and weighed it in his hand. 'The answer's in here. In the various statements, in your excellent report.'

'The – er – *answer*?' Joyce blinked polite disbelief. 'Excuse me, sir. But, do you mean the answer to the theft of the car? The answer to the burning of the car? The answer to the whereabouts of Garfield? The answer to ...'

'All the answers, Mr Joyce,' said Collins, calmly. 'They all dovetail. They're all in here.' He placed the file on his knee, and tapped it with a forefinger. He continued, 'Please – don't ask me to be specific, at this time ... I can't be. There's a stone out of place – a dovetail that doesn't quite fit ... more than that, I can't say.'

'In – er – in *there*?' Joyce nodded at the file on Collins's knee.

'In the statements. In the report. Somewhere.' Collins's lips moved into a slow smile, as he continued, 'Mr Joyce, you're a young man. Enthusiastic. An excellent policeman

... I don't doubt that, for one moment. But I have something you still lack. Service. And service – if you're prepared to accept it – brings experience. Colloquially, it's known as bobbying by the seat of the pants. Gut bobbying ... that's another expression. It's beyond explanation. It can't be accurately described. But – you have my solemn assurance – it exists.

'Consider ...' Collins paused, tasted the sherry, then went on, 'This crime – as far as you were concerned – was merely a missing, then burned out taxi. It necessitated the tracing of the man Garfield. Since then, we've put various pieces together and built part of the whole. That the disappearance of Garfield, and the burning of the taxi, are components of a slightly larger crime. That Hicks was part of that larger crime. That the crime, of necessity, was hurriedly conceived. That it was born of a football pool win, and that only a limited number of people could have known about that win ... known about that win, *and* known that the boy Emmerson attended Gladstone Comprehensive School.

'And, consider this ...' Once more Collins moistened his lips with sherry. 'Kidnapping. We must call it that, because it *is* that. But, what a puny ransom ... especially, these days. I know – it's almost all Emmerson won, but it still doesn't merit the risk of being caught and sentenced ... and, come to that, why not demand the whole thirty-two thousand? Why leave Emmerson two thousand, as a sort of "consolation prize"? The whole thing smacks of amateurism. It smacks of "gentlemanly conduct" ... of not kicking an opponent, when he's down. It smacks of desperation, and panic. The whole incident has a certain "feel" ... for want of a better expression, it has the hallmark of middle-class respectability, gone sour.

'Hicks ... we know he was neither middle-class nor res-

190

pectable. Garfield ... he's still something of an unknown quantity. Crowe – I think you're meeting him, later to-day ...'

'Half-ten, at *The Blue-Tailed Fly*,' said Joyce.

'Crowe,' said Collins, 'is approaching the enquiry from the Garfield angle. I'd like to approach it from the boy's angle.'

'The school?' asked Joyce.

'His form master. His headmaster. His classmates. Use your discretion. Take your statements, and your reports, as a starting point, and build on them. Double-check everything. The movement of the boy, from the time he left home, until the time he entered the taxi. Who did what. Who said what. Who saw what. Nothing too trivial ... and always remembering that *if* the boy told somebody about his father's pool win, that person is very unlikely to admit that knowledge.'

Joyce glanced at his wrist-watch, and said, 'It's just gone four, sir. After school hours.'

'There's a secretary – a Miss Benson ...'

'Ah!' A series of peculiar expressions flitted across Joyce's face.

Collins murmured, 'I beg your pardon?'

'Nothing, sir – er ... nothing.' Joyce finished the sherry, stood up, and said, 'Miss Benson should know their home addresses. I'll ask. I'll see as many as possible, before I meet Crowe.'

'Good.' Collins placed his glass on the military-chest table, then he stood up, and said, 'I'll keep the file, if I may. I'll contact Chief Superintendent Lennox ... then, if you don't mind, you can give Mr Crowe a lift back here, and we'll hold a council of war at – say – midnight. Will that be convenient?'

'Yes, sir. Quite convenient. And – er – thank you, sir.'

191

'Good luck, Mr Joyce,' smiled Collins. 'Good hunting.'


5.10 pm ......


Strictly speaking, the greengrocer's shop was closed. It had closed, for the day, ten minutes before, and the proprietor and his assistant – the girl called Judy – were performing their last tasks, before going home. The proprietor was listing the fruit and vegetables he'd need for the next day, while the girl was busying herself sweeping the floor of the shop.

The telephone bell rang, and a man's voice asked to speak with James Crowe ... 'He'll be across at Emmerson's house.'

The proprietor was mildly annoyed but, nevertheless, sent the girl across the road, to number forty-seven.

Crowe *was* there; he was enjoying a quick snack of cheese and biscuits, swilled down with strong, sweet tea.

He followed the girl back to the shop, walked into the rear room and picked up the receiver.

He said, 'Crowe, here.'

The voice was a man's voice. Muffled and, perhaps, disguised.

It said, 'Emmerson. Has he told you?'

'Things,' fenced Crowe.

'That we have his son?'

'Could be,' admitted Crowe, carefully.

'We deal with you, now.'

'Is that so?'

'The price is still thirty-thousand.'

'Man,' sneered Crowe, 'do you have an imagination!'

'Tell his father. We'll notify you of further details.'

'Such as?'

The phone went dead.

Crowe replaced the receiver, thanked the greengrocer and walked back across the street, in a brown study.

Something. *Something!* The choice of words. The choice of phrase. An ethereal thing which remained beyond his grasp. A gadfly. A Will o' the wisp.

Goddammit, the answer was there.

Somewhere ... *something.*

It was dark in the cave; dark, cold and becoming colder.

Garfield sat, hunched on a boulder, near the entrance to the cave. The youth was on another boulder, half-way towards the rear of the cave ... and the youth had almost worked his hands free of the nylon twine.

They hadn't exchanged conversation for some time.

Each had said all he had to say, and what remained was a silent embarrassment. The hostage–captor situation was, in some way, incomplete; it was – or so it seemed – impossible to suddenly replace friendship with hatred. Where there had once been mutual respect, there was now ... nothing.

The youth cleared his throat, before he broke the silence.

Then, he said, 'I'm hungry, Mr Garfield.'

'Yeah. Me, too.'

'We can't go all night, without food.'

'Sorry, Pete ... we've no choice. Tomorrow, maybe.'

'My head hurts,' complained the youth. 'Where Hicks hit me. It hurts, badly.'

'Hicks.' Garfield spoke the name with scorn-touched anger. With something not far from defeat. He stared out at the dark landscape, and said, 'Blame Hicks, son. For everything. It was never meant to be like this ... I swear.

We had food and comfort laid on. Nobody was going to hurt you. A short holiday – that's what it was going to be ... a short holiday for you, pending your father paying over the money. Now *this*.'

The evening grew thirty seconds older before the youth spoke again.

He said, 'A fire? Can't we light a fire? It's cold, Mr Garfield. We need a fire.'

'They'd spot it,' muttered Garfield.

'Who?'

'The police.'

The youth sounded surprised, when he said, 'The police won't be looking ... will they?'

'After Hicks's escapade,' sighed Garfield.

'Daddy won't have told them. I'm sure he won't.' The youth paused, then said, 'You *told* him not to tell them?'

'Yeah.'

'I guessed,' said the youth, then added, 'In that case he *won't* have told them.'

'Pete, they have him,' said Garfield, heavily. 'He was with Hicks. They'll have got it out of him. They'll know, by this time.'

'I don't think so.' The youth so obviously believed his words, and the belief rang in them, with the clarity of a perfectly tuned carillon. He urged, 'I *know*. If daddy gave his word, he'll keep it. He doesn't lie ... the police won't make him break his word.'

'Tomorrow, Pete ... tomorrow,' whispered Garfield.

What the whispered words meant, the youth couldn't understand. Only that they carried misery and defeat; that, although they included his name, they were not directed at *him*.

They were directed at something the youth had not yet experienced.

At a world which, by Garfield's yardstick, was sick unto death with the disease of corruption, greed and the worship of violence.


5.15 pm until 10.15 pm ...


James Crowe asked questions. He asked them of men, he asked them of women, and many of the people he questioned had already been interviewed by Joyce. Garfield's landlady, Garfield's friends, Garfield's passing acquaintances.

And the picture he built up was a contradiction.

There was (it seemed) no evil in the man. No trait of criminality. No hint of rottenness.

There was (or, again, so it seemed) a naïvety, almost beyond belief. Garfield was the champion of just about every lost cause under the sun; he was Peter Pan and Tinkerbell, rolled into one; it wasn't merely that he figured the world owed him a living, his beliefs went much farther than that – he figured the world owed *everybody* a living ... and the how-the-hell, and the why-the-hell was of no concern.

He was a nut case ... this, in the considered opinion of James Crowe.

He had been squeezed through the educational sausage-machine of a redbrick university, and managed a poor class B.A. but, in the course thereof, had become a part of every gathering of kinks which proliferate on the fringes of such establishments. He was all brain, but no reason. He knew all there was to know about theoretical perfection ... but knew damn-all about hard reality.

Within those few hours of investigation, Crowe lost count of the number of jobs Garfield had held ... sometimes for days, and never for more than a few weeks. From a porter at the local fruit market, to a stand-in arts master at half the schools of Bordfield. From a dishwasher, at almost every restaurant of the city, to a cataloguer at one of the private libraries. Dozens of jobs – scores of jobs ... and, always he'd given moderate satisfaction.

Nobody had disliked him but, on the other hand, nobody had become close enough to him to be a friend, in the real sense.

A happy-go-lucky nut case, beating out a perfectly good brain against candy-floss walls of multiple do-goodery.

And now, a *kidnapper*!

Detective Constable Randal Alexander Osbert Joyce was having similar difficulties. Getting to know what sort of a youth Peter Emmerson was. Gathering enough snippets of information upon which to base an assessment and, from that assessment, making a calculated guess concerning the person, or persons, with whom the youth might have shared a secret ... the secret of a football pool win.

Joyce spent the first hour of his enquiries with Miss Benson.

They sipped the inevitable tea, and he asked questions, but there was no hint of the previous evening's moment of copulation. They both knew, and they both remembered – of *course* they both remembered – but there was no awkwardness, and no embarrassment ... merely the closeness of old friends, as if the incident had been a substitute for a lifetime of mutual respect.

'What sort of a boy is he?' asked Joyce.

'A nice boy. Very polite, and very thoughtful.'

'The message about his father – the hoax – was he upset?'

'Oh, yes. Very.'

They'd been talking a good thirty minutes, before Joyce decided to take a chance.

He said, 'There's something I think you should know.'

'Really?' She leaned forward in her chair, slightly, clasped her fingers around the front of her knees, and smiled eager anticipation.

'It's very confidential,' said Joyce, quietly.

'Yes ... I see.'

'Even more than that. It's a secret.'

'Oh!'

'I'll have to ask you to give me your word, therefore. Not to mention it to anybody. Not to *anybody*.'

'You have my solemn assurance, Mr Joyce.'

Joyce took a deep breath, then said, 'The boy – the call from the hospital was a hoax, as you know – to get the boy into a taxi. I'm afraid the boy's been kidnapped.'

'Kidnapped!' She caught her breath. 'You mean ...'

'Kidnapped,' repeated Joyce, flatly. 'Being held for ransom.'

'But – but his father ... He's not a rich man. Is he? I mean, how can he ...'

'He recently won a prize on the pools.'

'Oh!'

'A fairly substantial amount.'

'Oh! ... I see.'

'Nobody was supposed to know. He didn't want publicity. But – obviously – somebody *did* know. The ransom demanded fits in with the amount Emmerson's won.'

'That's – that's *awful*.' She was almost breathless at the wickedness of which she'd been told. 'I mean ... It's – it's ... *awful*.'

Joyce nodded, and gave her time to accustom herself to the news.

Then, he said, 'My job – my side of the enquiry – is to

find out who the boy might have told. About the win, I mean. His pals. People at school. Anybody. Just who else knew about the win.'

'And,' she ended the progression for him, 'who knew it was worthwhile kidnapping him.'

'Quite,' said Joyce.

A smile touched her lips, as she said, 'Me, for example?'

'Good Lord!' The possibility shocked Joyce. He said, 'Did *you* know?'

'No.' She shook her head. 'But you have to ask me ... obviously.'

'We-ell ... no. That is to say ...'

'Of course you had to ask me,' she said, gently. 'I've answered. I've told you I didn't know. But, *had* I known, I'd have denied it ... wouldn't I?'

'Look – Miss Benson ...'

'Agatha, please.'

'Agatha ... there are certain people who are above suspicion.'

'Thank you.'

'If I'd thought for a moment – if I'd even contemplated the *possibility* – would I have told you about the kidnapping?'

'I don't know. Perhaps.' She pondered the question for a moment, then said, 'No ... I suppose not.'

'So, you see, Miss – er – Agatha,' said Joyce, 'we have to go backwards. In reverse, as it were. To get everything. Everything! Do you understand?'

'Ye-es,' said Miss Benson. 'I think so.'

'Right ... now, you put the boy in the taxi?'

'Yes.'

'And, as I understand things, he recognised the man Garfield.'

'Yes. They spoke to each other.'

198

'And, before that, the boy was where?'

'In the school. I took him to the school, from the headmaster's study.'

'And, before that?'

'You mean the boy?'

'Yes.'

'He was in his classroom. It was T.D. period, and he ...'

'T.D.?'

'Technical Drawing.'

'Oh, I see.'

'I was with Mr Denning – we were discussing certain overlaps in the scheduled periods – and the headmaster sent for me.'

'And?'

'Well, then he told me. The headmaster, I mean ... about the phone call we thought had come from the hospital. So, I brought the boy Emmerson, from his classroom.'

'From T.D.?'

'Yes, from T.D. – from Mr Finchley's classroom ... he's in Mr Finchley's class. I brought him to the headmaster's study. After I'd telephoned for the taxi.'

'You telephoned for the taxi first?'

'Yes.'

'Then you brought the boy to the headmaster's study?'

'Yes.'

'Where, presumably, he waited, until the arrival of the taxi.'

'Yes, that's right.'

'And you, too, waited. In the headmaster's study. Until the arrival of the taxi?'

'Yes ... of course.'

Joyce worked very conscientiously. Step by step, minute by minute, inch by inch. Backwards through remembered time, until they reached the moment when Agatha Benson had left her home, the previous day, for Gladstone Comprehensive School. And every step was noted, every minute itemised and every inch recorded in Joyce's notebook.

Each name mentioned was underlined and, each time a name was mentioned, an address was asked for, and was given.

Which meant that Detective Constable Joyce spent a very busy evening.

He visited each address, verified, checked and re-checked everything Agatha Benson had told him and, by the time he figured Crowe should be waiting, at *The Blue-Tailed Fly*, he could put his hand on his heart and say he damn near knew the pulse-beat of Peter Emmerson for the two hours before he was kidnapped.

Meanwhile, the youth was indulging in a little self-help.

His hands were free. They were sore and chafed, where the nylon twine had resisted – they were even bleeding a little – but they were no longer bound.

The cave was cold; a few degrees of frost cold. But (from what the youth could see) Garfield was impervious to the cold. Garfield still sat on the boulder, by the cave entrance; hunched forward, with his head in his hands and his elbows resting on his knees, and not moving. As immobile as a statue ... a statue of despair, silhouetted against a cloudless night sky, a brilliant half-moon and a dusting of stars. Dark, against a lesser darkness. Unseeing and unknowing.

For a moment, the youth felt pity. He moved his freed fingers to ease the cramp, and get the circulation flowing properly and, for a moment, he contemplated one last appeal to sanity.

Then, he remembered his father, and the pity was replaced by anger.

He eased himself upright and moved slowly forward.

Testing each step, in case a loose stone might give away his secret. Ensuring that what faint shadow the moonlight gave him, didn't touch his hunched jailer. He stopped, bent his knees and reached forward to pick up the slab of limestone Garfield had used as a silent threat, when the youth had required to urinate. With equal care, he straightened his legs, grasped his primitive weapon in his right hand and, once more, approached the man who held him captive.

As the stone swung, the youth's foot slipped, slightly, on a pebble, and Garfield raised his head and began to turn ... but it was too late. The stone, aimed in a side-swipe at the side of the head, caught Garfield above the brows and opened a gash wide enough to expose bone.

Garfield toppled, and the youth stooped and, three more times, brought the stone down, hard, on the unconscious man's skull.

Then, the youth threw away the blood-marked stone, stepped from the cave ... and ran.

The time was exactly 10.15 pm.

10.15 pm ......

'Jamaica?' asked Crowe.

'Spanish Town,' replied the girl.

'And now this?' Crowe glanced around the garish interior of *The Blue-Tailed Fly*, glanced at the brief, white panties and the even briefer, white halter, and added, 'And *this*.'

'It's a living, man,' said the girl, defensively.

'Some living!'

The coloured girl looked cross and sulky. She moved to

her position, behind the tiny counter, and said, 'You wanna check in a hat, or some other thing, mister. That's what I get paid for ... that's all.'

'That,' agreed Crowe, 'and getting the customers a hard on ... *that's* what you get paid for, sweetie. Okay – kid yourself, a little ... but don't kid me.'

'Look – what the hell ...'

'Nic,' interrupted Crowe, drily, 'gives you a good write-up, honey. But, Nic ain't too well up on the facts of life. Right?'

'Nic?' Dinah Lemmings, the coloured hat-check of *The Blue-Tailed Fly*, stared half-disbelief at Crowe. 'You telling me you know Nic?'

'Yeah.' Crowe nodded, as he reached for cigarettes and lighter. 'A nice guy ... and in big trouble.'

'I – er – I heard things,' she said, quietly.

'That,' observed Crowe, 'is just about the biggest horse-fart I've heard for some time.'

'You meaning something, man?' The girl's eyes blazed.

'Yeah. I'm meaning something.'

'Just *what*?'

'We-ell, now ...' Crowe lighted a cigarette, and returned the lighter to his pocket, as he said, 'You and the creep who runs this sewer. That's what I mean, honey.'

'I don't catch the crazy talk,' sneered the girl.

'And a germ called Hicks. Who – fortunately for all concerned – is now helping some mortician to meet his overheads.'

'Get lost, coloured man. I'm not with you ... and I ain't gonna run to catch up.'

'And another guy,' continued Crowe. 'Name of Garfield ... he gets a kick outa burning taxis.'

'Blow, man ... eh? You ain't said one word ...'

'And lifting kids. Kids like Pete Emmerson.'

She closed her mouth, then opened it again as the impact of Crowe's words drove home.

'You neck-and-neck now, honey?' asked Crowe, gently.

'No,' she breathed. 'I still don't get things, but ...'

'A lift.' Crowe's voice became cold, and threatening. 'Nic's kid's been snatched ... or am I telling yesterday's news?'

'I – I didn't know.' she breathed.

'You're a sweet little liar,' he accused.

'No! I swear to God ...'

'You knew about the pools win, honey.'

'Pools win? What pools ...'

'Bread, sweetie. Nice thick slices.'

'I – I didn't know.'

'The creep who runs this clip-house knew.'

'Oh!'

'From you, kid.'

'No ... not from me.'

'From you,' insisted Crowe.

'I swear.' The girl looked scared. Worried. She said, 'I like Nic. He keeps his paws to himself. He treats me like I'm human.'

'Ain't we all ... more, or less,' mocked Crowe.

'He – he said he was gonna retire. That's all. That he was gonna retire.'

'What with? A begging-bowl?'

'He – he didn't say. Just that – y'know ... he looked kinda happy. Excited.'

'And you mentioned it ... eh?' sneered Crowe. 'To the Quincey punk.'

'No – I ...' She paused, then said, 'Yeah ... maybe. We got to talking, one day. One day, last week.'

'Talking?' Crowe's lip curled.

'Mister,' said the girl, heavily, 'with Quincey, you do one

of two things ... and the one I dislike least is talking.'

'About Nic.'

'About any damn thing ... just to keep his mind off the other.'

'About Nic,' repeated Crowe, coldly.

'Something. Some damn thing.' The girl looked defeated. Beaten. She muttered, 'Hey, man, you don't know. You do not *know*! With that pig, you just talk, and talk, and talk ... or else you screw. I said something. Nic retiring ... I said something about that. What else? Nic had knocked his gums about it. He hadn't said not to say ... so, what was wrong? It wasn't no big secret. It wasn't no ...' She stopped looked into Crowe's face, and said, 'Man, do you have any notion? This place? The animals who come to this menagerie? Some of 'em are two steps down from nothing. Their whole world ... legs, tits and pussy.'

'My heart bleeds, kid,' murmured Crowe. 'Remind me to buy you a new G-string.'

A voice from behind Crowe growled, 'Talking about bleeding, nigger.'

And Crowe turned, joyfully, to meet trouble, head-on.

The hat-check counter was in the foyer of the club, and the foyer sported expensive purple carpet and matching wallpaper. The hidden lighting, although subdued, gave illumination to framed pictures of nudes in exotic postures and, under each picture, a one-armed bandit, or a pin-table, stood ready to receive the small change, prior to the customer entering into the frolicsome process of being completely fleeced. The openings from the foyer were doorway-sized arches, each hung with purple drapes and, beyond the drapes, the mutter and sounds of movement told of another busy night at *The Blue-Tailed Fly*.

The speaker was Quincey, himself, and he was flanked by a duo of tuxedo-dressed bouncers.

Quincey snapped, 'Out, black boy. You're soiling the carpet.'

Crowe smiled, in anticipation. He balanced on the soles of his sneakers, and loosened his shoulders under the windcheater.

'You going?' said Quincey.

Crowe smiled, and said, 'I'm waiting to be put, bastard.'

Quincey nodded, and the two bouncers moved forward.

Crowe did the unexpected. Instead of retreating, he stepped sideways, then forward and, as he drew level with the right-hand bouncer, he linked his fingers into a two-handed fist, turned and hammered the bouncer across the nape of the neck.

The bouncer gave a single grunt, before his knees buckled.

Quincey stood between Crowe and the second bouncer, and Crowe grabbed Quincey by the back of the collar and the seat of the pants, lifted him clear of the floor and, virtually, hit the second bouncer in the face with the top of Quincey's head, battering-ram fashion.

Crowe was still upright, and wasn't even breathing heavily.

Quincey and his two gladiators were sprawling and holding their various hurts.

The bruiser who had stopped the rabbit-punch hauled himself to his hands and knees. Crowe swivelled on the ball of his left foot, glanced over his right shoulder, to check the aiming point, then back-heeled the unfortunate bruiser in the nape of the neck with his right foot. Once more the bruiser went down. This time, he stayed down.

Quincey scrambled to his feet and rushed for the coloured man's back.

Crowe sensed, rather than saw, the attack from the rear. He crouched, like a sprinter on starting-blocks and, when Quincey stumbled forward over the bent back, Crowe grabbed one of the flailing arms, pulled and jerked himself upright. One of Quincey's shoes actually punched a hole in the ceiling plaster, before he ended his flight draped across one of the pin-table machines.

Crowe turned to meet the last of the three ... and, this time, it wasn't fancy. He blocked a right swing, which damn near had a postcard attached, and sunk his own right fist, wrist-deep into the bruiser's gut. Then, as the bruiser folded forward, he positioned the head, with a gentle left, before slamming a right, dead centre, at the bruiser's nose. From then, on, the bruiser was fighting blind; the streaming tears made the rest of Crowe's job easy. He either blocked, or weaved away from, windmill haymakers while, at the same time exploding lefts and rights onto the bruiser's battered features, with a timing and a fury which rocked the head on a neck which seemed to be made of tyre-rubber. It was a good, old-fashioned, scientific shellacking and gradually, almost like a sinking ship, the bouncer's legs wobbled and he crumpled, and hadn't the energy left to lift himself from the carpet.

Crowe was panting a little as he grinned at the hat-check girl.

'Nice work-out, mister,' she said, flat-voiced. 'But, come tomorrow, who you figure's gonna foot the bill?'

The grin stayed in place, as he said, 'You pick rough friends, honey. Don't squeal if they ain't always polite.'

Before the girl could answer a newcomer arrived.

He stopped at the entrance, surveyed the battlefield and cocked an eye at the conqueror.

He said, 'Pardon me, but am I needed here?'

'Who knows?' countered Crowe.

'I'm a police officer ... if that helps to answer your question.'

Crowe's grin broadened, as he said, 'My name's Crowe.'

'I suggest,' murmured Joyce, 'that we leave, together ...
now. Before somebody insists upon making an official complaint.'


11 pm ......


Crowe and Joyce were both a couple of sizes above average,
and it was somewhat cramped in the Mini-Cooper.
Cramped, but cosy. They were ahead of schedule, therefore
Joyce had parked in a lay-by, between Bordfield and Less-
ford, and now they were exchanging small-talk as they
gradually learned to know each other.
  'Collins,' said Joyce, apropos of nothing in particular.
  'Nice guy,' murmured Crowe. 'They don't come bigger.'
  'He has a reputation.'
  'Uhuh. It follows.'
  'As a policeman.'
  'Yeah.'
  'As something of a cold fish.'
  Crowe said, 'That ain't so, friend.'
  'No?' Joyce sounded surprised.
  'I've known him a long time.'
  'Really.'
  'From the war. He was my skipper.'
  'Navy?'
  'Lancasters. Five Bomber Group. He chauffeured us to
the target, and back, lots of times.'
  'Really ... I didn't know.'
  'Lots of things,' said Crowe, softly.
  'What?'
  'People don't know about him.'

'Yes. I suppose so ... as with most people.'

Crowe stared through the windscreen, and said, 'I seen that guy weep, once ... after Dresden.'

'The war?' enquired Joyce, with only marginal interest.

'Dresden,' repeated Crowe, sadly.

'I've read about it.'

'We didn't read it, man.' Crowe's voice was soft. Savage, and filled with disgust. 'We *made* it.'

'Really.'

'That was Old Man Churchill's raid,' mused Crowe. 'No military target ... y'know that, man? Nothing! No flack. A few fighters ... nothing to bring a sweat on. But *some* raid. That was a terror raid, man. Just that. Not one damn thing else. To show Stalin ... eh? What we *could* do. To ease his cork back into the bottle, supposing he had any ideas about not stopping when Hitler was finished. We figured ... that was the only reason for that damn raid. And civilian casualties? ... y'know how many, man? They ain't yet worked 'em out. All these years ... and they're still guessing. But, bigger than Hiroshima. That they *do* know. That they *ain't* guessing. That damn town – oh, Jesus! ... I sat in the turret. I watched it, when it was over. Y'know ... a blow-torch! That was Dresden, man. A town turned into a blow-torch. No man on that raid is ever gonna forget. *Ever.*

'And, man, they apologised ... y'know – apologised. They sent the boffins round, to explain things to us. They had a name for it. A Fire Storm. You get a town burning hot enough, it pushes the air up. Winds come in – in from all sides – to replace the air ... and that adds oxygen to the fires, and makes 'em blaze bigger. So more air goes up ... and faster. And more wind comes in ... and faster. Man, they clocked gales of one hundred miles an hour, coming in – from every direction – feeding that fire ... one bloody

208

great fire. You end up with a blow-torch. Only, it ain't a blow-torch. It's a town, with people – with women and kids ... a town called Dresden, turned into a Fire Storm.'

Crowe stopped speaking for a moment. He dragged deep on his cigarette, then muttered, 'We made that raid, friend. Collins up front. Me in the arse-end turret. From then on, it didn't matter. We flew more raids – lots more raids ... and, after Dresden, we didn't give a damn whether we made it or not. After Dresden we *deserved* to die ... and we still ain't fit to live.'

They smoked their cigarettes, in silence.

Then Joyce switched on the ignition, guided the car from the lay-by and headed towards Lessford.

12.10 am ......

The answer, when it came, was so obvious – so beautifully complete – that, of the four men seated comfortably in the main room of the flat, three felt like kicking themselves.

It was foolproof – it was water-tight – and it had been staring them in the face for more than twelve hours. Get the burned-out taxi right, know about the kidnapping, and there *was* only one answer.

Lennox blew out his cheeks, ruffled the wisps of hair above his right ear, treated himself to a Cheshire-cat leer, then rumbled, 'Henry, old cock, there ain't no justice in this world. You should never have been *allowed* to leave the force.'

Joyce gazed near-hero-worship at the slim, ex-chief super-intendent, and breathed, 'Christ! ... as easy as *that*.'

Crowe contented himself with a quiet, 'Thanks, skipper.'

Each man took the news in his own way, but each man knew he'd witnessed policing reduced to mathematical pre-cision ... that there was a case to answer and, already, enough to merit an arrest.

Simple?

We-ell, in later years, when the pro's and con's of the con-viction were debated by after-the-event knowledgeable types, while the midnight canteen tea grew cold and skim-med, it was openly admitted that the list of possible suspects *was* on the short side. Half a dozen – certainly no more than half a dozen ... but, come to that, one hell of a lot of crimes remain on the books, marked 'Undetected', despite the certain knowledge that the culprit *must* be one of a mere handful. That isn't good enough. Two is one too many.

And, when the canteen scuttlebutt had all been spouted – when the latter-day masterminds had all had their say – the simple fact remained ... that Collins had, almost off-handedly, aimed his arrow of accusation and scored the only gold on the butt.

'That's it, then.' Lennox heaved himself from the comfort of the wing-chair. 'We'll have him in. This time o' night ... beautiful. He'll still have the dew on his rose. D'you mind if I use your phone, Henry?'

'Not at all.' Collins waved a languid hand towards the telephone, on the side-table.

As if it had been waiting for the gesture, the bell of the instrument rang.

Collins strolled across the room, lifted the receiver from its rest and answered the call.

He held the receiver out, for the fat detective, and said, 'It's for you, Lenny.'

The others listened to half of a telephone conversation, and saw Lennox's face light up with delight.

He said, 'Lennox here ...... Good God! Is that a fact? D' you know where it is ? ...... Champion. Get a squad car out there, pronto. Pick him up, and bring him in to Bordfield Headquarters. We'll be there, before he is ...... Oh, aye. You'd better get a medic, on tap, to check that he's in one piece. And pass word to the squad car, to tell him we'll have his uncle waiting for him.'

Lennox lowered the receiver onto its rest, beamed delight at the other three men, and said, 'Young Emmerson. He's slipped Garfield. He's at some God-forsaken farm, some-

where ... waiting to be picked up. He phoned in, to Bordfield. That's it, folks. That's what I call a *good* ending.'


I am ......


The man denied it ... but, what else?

Lennox leaned forward across his posh desk, and roared,
'Damn it to hell, man. We *know*.'

'Don't be ridiculous.' The man's lips moved into a con-
temptuous sneer. 'You tell me the boy's been kidnapped.
I must, I suppose, accept that ... unless, of course, this is
some involved bluff. But, to suggest that *I* had a hand in the
kidnapping isn't merely outrageous. It's pathetic. Heaven
knows what rank you hold ...'

'Detective chief superintendent.'

'In which case, the rising crime rate is quite understand-
able.'

'Don't get *too* stroppy, old cock,' warned Lennox, coldly.
'Not in this office ... we're playing on *my* ground, here.'

'Threats?'

'Advice,' growled Lennox. 'We reduce steel bars to iron
filings, in this place ... and never forget it.'

'Such a childish remark,' mocked the man. He began
to straighten from the chair, and continued, 'I have a bed
waiting. I can't waste time ...'

'Siddown!'

Lennox glanced at Joyce, and the D.C. moved a couple
of steps to his left, and took up a position at the door of
the office.

The man murmured, 'I'm too old to be bullied,' but,
nevertheless, re-seated himself on the chair.

Lennox rubbed the side of his face, meditatively, then rumbled, 'We don't really *need* a confession.'

'In that case ...'

'But it makes for tidy bobbying.'

'Dear me. You must spend half your life ...'

'And I'm all for tidy bobbying.'

'... being disappointed.'

'I do.' Lennox nodded, ponderously. 'But, not this time, cocky. This time ...' He bent his mouth into a quick, wolfish grin, before he growled, 'Henry, old son, take this smarmy bastard to pieces for me, will you? Skin him alive ... let's have a decko at the wheels going round.'

'If you think ...' began the man.

'My dear sir, nothing. Nothing, at all.' Collins eased himself onto centre-stage, hooked a thigh over a corner of the desk and, as he fitted a cigarette into his briar holder, said, 'Mr Lennox has a certain turn of phrase.'

'I'm a slob,' agreed Lennox, cheerfully.

'He tends to be over-exuberant.'

'I'm an oaf.'

'He is slightly pleonastic.'

'What the hell *that* means.'

'But,' continued Collins, as he touched the end of the cigarette with a lighter flame, 'if we might now be a little more concise.'

'Nothing would please me more,' said the man, stiffly.

'Good ... good.' Collins smiled. 'May we, then, start with certain facts. The boy – Peter Emmerson – *has* been kidnapped.'

'I'll accept that,' said the man. 'You state it as a fact ... I accept it. But ...'

'Kidnapped, by a gentleman by the name of Garfield – Leonard Garfield – the driver of a taxi.'

The man nodded acknowledgement of the statement.

'Garfield drove the taxi to Gladstone Comprehensive School, to pick up the boy Emmerson ... as a direct result of a false message, in which it was reported that Emmerson's father had met with an accident, been injured and was at the City Hospital.'

'If you say so,' agreed the man.

'You have my word,' murmured Collins.

'In that case, I see no reason to doubt you.'

'Good.' Collins drew on the cigarette and exhaled a cloud of smoke at the ceiling. Without lowering his eyes, he said, 'A lie, of course – the story of his father's injury, I mean ... and every lie must be backed up by other lies. Agreed?'

'An adage. But, not always true.'

They reminded Lennox of class knife-fighters. Evenly matched. Circling each other, and watching for an opening. Crouched and balanced, each with his thumb along the blade of his steel, each feinting before dancing back from the probing slash of his opponent. They reminded Lennox very much of class knife-fighters, and he watched and listened, and hoped to God Collins carried that little extra class.

'The ransom,' drawled Collins, 'was based upon a win on the football pools.'

'Really?' The man pretended bored surprise.

'Thirty thousand pounds.'

'Quite a modest sum ... surely?'

'Only if you have it.'

'Quite.'

'And, of course, if you know it's available.'

'Of course.'

'Tell me.' Collins once more inhaled smoke from his cigarette. He allowed the question to leave his lips, gift-wrapped in tobacco smoke. 'Did *you* know about the pools win?'

214

'It might be construed as an admission,' countered the man.

'That you knew about a pools win?' mocked Collins, gently.

'No ... I suppose not,' said the man, grudgingly. He hesitated, then said, 'Yes. I knew about the win. It was fairly common knowledge. These things always are.'

It was first blood to Collins. Only a scratch ... but it had drawn scarlet. The man had known – despite the 'No Publicity' warranty ... a warranty of which he wasn't aware.

'Hicks,' murmured Collins.

'Hicks? Hicks?' The man frowned his concentration, then said, 'The name rings a bell. Something recently ...'

'He killed a policeman.'

'Ah, yes. He was ...'

'He was in the kidnapping conspiracy.'

'Was he, indeed? It wasn't mentioned.'

'Where?'

'In the newspapers. On the radio.'

'Hicks. Garfield. And, yourself,' said Collins, dreamily.

'I don't know ...'

'At the moment – at *this* moment – the boy, Emmerson, is downstairs, in the canteen. With his uncle. He broke captivity ... he broke away from Garfield.'

Very deliberately, the man said, 'I don't know Hicks.'

It was an obvious change. An obvious cover-up. He'd been going to say 'I don't know Garfield' – and both Lennox and Joyce *knew* that had been his intention – but Collins's timed interruption had forced him to substitute the name 'Hicks'.

Call it a knife-fight, and the substitution represented a split-second weave to avoid what could have been a fatal thrust.

'But you know *Garfield*,' said Collins.

'I know a young radical called Garfield,' admitted the man, carefully.

'A part-time taxi driver.'

'Is he? I wouldn't know.'

'He drove the taxi.'

'Yes ... you've already said.'

'What do you know about taxi firms?' asked Collins innocently.

The man smiled, and said, 'I haven't made a study of them.'

'That, I can well believe.' Collins returned smile for smile.

The man removed the smile from his face, and said, 'What's that supposed to mean?'

'You see,' mused Collins, 'it had to be *that* taxi.'

'I don't ...'

'Driven by *that* man.'

'I still don't ...'

'Otherwise, the thing wouldn't have worked,' explained Collins. 'Any other taxi – any other taxi firm – any other driver ... and the kidnapping wouldn't have been possible.'

'Ye-es ... I can see that,' admitted the man.

'Radio taxis.' Collins continued his musings. 'The one used was a radio taxi. The whole escapade revolved around it being a radio taxi.'

'Did it?' said the man and, if anything, his tone conveyed boredom.

'Will you follow my logic, please?' asked Collins, politely.

'I'll try,' promised the man.

'Ten minutes to eleven, Monday morning. Garfield had just arrived at the taxi firm. He was sent on a call, from fifteen Fairfax Avenue ... to take a party called Chambers, from that address to the bus depot. A simple, straight-forward call ... agreed?'

'So it would seem.'

'Indeed – so it *did* seem ... except that there isn't a fifteen Fairfax Avenue. Nor is there anybody living in that district called Chambers.'

'A mistake,' said the man. 'A mistaken name ... or a mistaken address. Perhaps both. It has been known.'

'Quite,' agreed Collins. 'But Garfield didn't report the mistake. As far as the taxi firm was concerned, it was a legitimate call, which had been attended to, and Garfield was available for any other calls. He was on the streets. Handy.'

'I really don't see what you're ...'

'Handy,' continued Collins, 'for a call which he received from a certain Miss Benson ... at twenty minutes past eleven. To go to Gladstone Comprehensive School, and pick up a pupil. Peter Emmerson.'

'You mean Miss Benson ...'

'Oh, come now!' Impatience suddenly made Collins's voice hard, and cold. 'You're a relatively intelligent man. It *had* to be Garfield. Otherwise the kidnapping couldn't be committed. More than that, Garfield had to be handy – available ... which is why the false Fairfax Avenue took him out on the streets. Miss Benson telephoned ... but *you* gave her the number. Nor did you look it up in the directory. When Miss Benson entered your office you'd just replaced the phone – or so it seemed ... more play-acting. All that rubbish about a call from the City Hospital. You received no such call ...'

'It's already been established. It was a hoax. It was ...'

'Emmerson didn't call it a hoax. When he visited your office, *he* didn't call it a hoax. Only you. You've always called it a hoax. It *was* ... a double hoax. It was never even made.'

In a last, hopeless defence, Adams said, 'I know the number of City Taxis. I've used them, before. Often. I *know* their number.'

'And the telephone number of the greengrocer?' snapped Collins.

'I beg your pardon?'

'In Christopher Crescent? *That* number? You phoned it – when you contacted Crowe ... we three, Miss Benson and yourself. Nobody else was told that Crowe was staying at Emmerson's home. That he might be contacted via the greengrocer. None of us phoned ... and it was a man's voice.'

'In-indeed.' It was a verbal stumble; as if he'd stubbed the toe of his tongue on an uneven word as he staggered around looking for a possible way out of the maze.

'*Al*,' sneered Lennox.

'What?'

'The lad told us. Garfield ... he's one of those matey types. Always shortening names. Very palsy-walsy. He's well known for it ... *Al*.'

'Aldous Frederick Adams,' added Collins.

'You must understand that it was necessary. That is to say, it *became* necessary.' Adams's composure held. His voice was quite calm. Quite controlled, and not at all like the voice of a kidnapper. 'My salary isn't all it might be. It's ridiculous, in fact, bearing in mind the cost of living and the responsibility I carry. And this girl – she's more of a young woman, in fact – she flouted herself in front of me ... and I was human enough to be weak. A Miss Black. Not a pleasant story, gentlemen. Sordid, but not uncommon. And now, her father insists upon an abortion ... and abortions cost money. Under-the-counter abortions, I mean.

And, when Finchley – that's Emmerson's form-master –
told me, in strictest confidence, about the pools win ...
Emmerson having told *him*, in strictest confidence ...'

'Feeling better?' asked Crowe.

The youth smiled, and nodded, then said, 'I'd like to go
see daddy, now.'

'Tomorrow,' promised Crowe. 'You're the tonic he needs,
but he'll be asleep at this hour ... which is what you
should be.'

'What are they doing upstairs?' asked the youth.

'Talking.' Crowe stood up from the Formica-topped
table and collected the beakers and plates, prior to return-
ing them to the canteen hatch.

When Crowe returned to the table, the youth asked,
'Who are they talking to?'

'A guy,' said Crowe. 'The guy responsible for all this.'

'Do I know him?' asked the youth.

'Yeah. But, it makes no matter ... you'll learn soon
enough. Only, just remember one thing, Pete. He's white
– white, and pretty important – you're black ... but that
ain't making things any easier for him.'

'Why *should* it?' The youth's eyes widened a little.

'You keep thinking that, Pete,' said Crowe, gently. 'You
keep thinking that – asking that question ... and make
sure you always get the answer right.'

As they walked from the canteen, the youth said, 'Mr
Garfield. I'm worried. I hit him as hard as I could.'

'Yeah.' Crowe rested a guiding hand on the youth's
shoulder. 'Sleep easy, son. He'll be okay.'

2.35 pm ......


But Crowe was wrong.

They found the cave, with the help of the youth, and much searching and, when they found the cave they also found the body of Garfield.

The verdict of a subsequent Coroner's Inquest was Death by Misadventure, due to a head injury, followed by prolonged exposure.

But, that day – at a few minutes after 2.30 pm, when they first saw the body – the youth wept in memory of a friendship which, of necessity, had had to be destroyed.

'I killed him,' he sniffled. 'I didn't mean to ... but I killed him.'

'The weather killed him, old son,' comforted Lennox. 'It's obvious. That's what the verdict'll be. The weather. And *he* chose the spot ... not you. He chose to break the law. To become a criminal. All along the line, old son, it was *his* choice. What you did you'd every right to do. *He* was the nasty, not you.'

'You didn't know him,' muttered the youth.

'No ... but I know what he was a part of.'

'He wasn't like Hicks.'

'As bad.'

'*No!*' The youth turned, to defend the dead Garfield. He almost shouted, 'He was my friend. My *friend*! All he wanted was some money. That's all. He didn't want to hurt me. But, you can't understand that, can you? Because you're a – you're a ...'

He ran down the slope, from the cave and towards the parked police cars.

'A copper.' Crowe ended the sentence the youth hadn't been able to end. He sighed, then said, 'Man ... this is gonna take generations.'

Joyce was there, too, and Joyce added, 'From both sides.'